T4-APV-079

OTHER BOOKS BY HAMPTON STONE

THE SWINGER WHO SWUNG BY THE NECK
THE CORPSE WAS NO BARGAIN AT ALL
THE FUNNIEST KILLER IN TOWN
THE KID WAS LAST SEEN HANGING TEN
THE REAL SERENDIPITOUS KILL
THE BABE WITH THE TWISTABLE ARM
THE MAN WHO LOOKED DEATH IN THE EYE
THE MAN WHO WAS THREE JUMPS AHEAD
THE GIRL WHO KEPT KNOCKING THEM DEAD
THE STRANGLER WHO COULDN'T LET GO
THE MAN WHO HAD TOO MUCH TO LOSE
THE CORPSE WHO HAD TOO MANY FRIENDS
THE CORPSE THAT REFUSED TO STAY DEAD
THE MURDER THAT WOULDN'T STAY SOLVED
THE NEEDLE THAT WOULDN'T HOLD STILL
THE GIRL WITH THE HOLE IN HER HEAD
THE CORPSE IN THE CORNER SALOON

The Kid Who Came

Home With a Corpse

AN INNER SANCTUM MYSTERY BY

HAMPTON STONE

SIMON AND SCHUSTER · NEW YORK

PUBLISHED BY SIMON AND SCHUSTER
ROCKEFELLER CENTER, 630 FIFTH AVENUE
NEW YORK, NEW YORK 10020

FIRST PRINTING

SBN 671–21174–9
LIBRARY OF CONGRESS CATALOG CARD NUMBER: 70-189544
DESIGNED BY EVE METZ
MANUFACTURED IN THE UNITED STATES OF AMERICA
BY THE BOOK PRESS, BRATTLEBORO, VERMONT

For
Salvatore Ragghianti
Frater, ave atque vale

1

SOMETIMES I think it might not be a bad idea if a man in the DA's office could go through life alone. No friends. No acquaintances. I'm not going to say that every person I've ever known has taken a turn at pitching me head first into a boiling pot of grief, but that is the way it's gone more often than anyone could like. When a double dose of hell comes winging at me and it's been occasioned by a good friend, I can tell myself that one must take the rough with the smooth and that maybe the well-known blessings of friendship do compensate for its headaches.

When, however, I catch several kinds of hell because of someone I hardly even know, I ask myself what compensates then. Bashings and stompings seem an excessive price to pay for a few courteous greetings and some occasional exchanges of perfunctory remarks along the mahogany of the Club bar. Ralph Henderson was an acquaintance. He was a fellow member of the Club but he had never been one of my cronies. He was an agreeable face, a pleasant smile, a look of worry around the eyes. He was also pin-striped suits, conservative ties, and consistently unstartling opinions, whether on the subject of politics or on the pennant races.

I didn't even know his name. When he dropped in on me one day and the kid from the outer office brought me his card, I read the name off without recognition.

"Ralph Henderson," I muttered. "Did he ask for me specifically?"

"He asked for you, sir. He said a personal call. He said he's a friend of yours."

I went back to studying the card, but further scrutiny of its neat engraving didn't make the name any more familiar. A forgotten friend? It seemed unlikely. You know somebody, but you've let him slip your mind. If you are reminded of him, you can't come up with anything more definite than "that tall guy, Whatsisname," but then the minute you're told, it does come back to you. You've known it all along. You had just mislaid it. On this one, however, I was reading his name and nothing was coming back.

"You're sure he wants me? You didn't get the name wrong?"

"His name? It's on the card. Mr. Henderson. Isn't that what's on his card?"

"Henderson. Right. I meant my name. He could be asking for someone else."

"I know your name, sir. He asked for you."

If you go out of the cubicle I share with Assistant District Attorney Jeremiah X. Gibson and you turn the corner of the corridor, there's a spot from which you can see a sizeable segment of the outer office. If your man happens to be waiting in that segment, you can look him over before you've involved yourself with him. Often enough you're lucky. He's waiting where you want him and he's not keeping any watchful eye on the corridor. You can look him over and not yourself be seen.

Henderson couldn't have been better placed for me to have a look at him. He also couldn't have been better placed for turning it about. He was planted there in the outer office at the end of the corridor and he looked as eager and alert as a cat at a mouse hole. He had me spotted the minute I came around the corner; and by the time I had made that almost instantaneous adjustment that says, "Oh, that guy. This is the way he would look when he doesn't have a drink in his hand," he was already loping down the corridor toward me, hand extended and face split wide open in grinning friendliness.

Within an instant he was all over me with booming warmth and old-buddy pawings.

"Mac, you old rascal," he roared, capturing my hand the while and squeezing it hard enough to cripple it.

Since he had never before had my hand in his, I had no way of knowing whether the man was a congenital bone crusher or the handshake was part of a program for taking me by storm. He kept my hand in his, leaving me nothing but the alternatives of letting him go on holding it or retrieving it by slugging him into submission with my still free left. Furthermore he didn't stop with the handshake. He also brought his left hand into play, closing it around my arm and setting it to kneading my biceps. Just as I had him tagged for a masseur on a busman's holiday, he turned the biceps loose, made a fist of his left, and clouted me playfully on the shoulder. Then, even as his hand bounced off my shoulder, he opened it out flat to fetch me a resounding slap on the back and as quickly followed that by flinging his arm around me and crushing me to him in a jovial hug. He could have been welcoming me back into the huddle just after I'd scored the winning touchdown in the final seconds of play. On the other hand it was more as though I had merely squeezed out a tie. After all, he didn't kiss me.

Let's face it. I'm a social coward. I can't pretend otherwise. I didn't have the heart to leave the man with all this affectionate athleticism of his hanging out in a vacuum. I couldn't quite respond in kind, but I did make a stab at cordiality.

"Ralph, you old such-and-such," I chortled. "What brings you down to this neck of the woods?"

Maybe I don't talk the world's most brilliant dialogue, but you've got to give me this much. Ordinarily I do better than that, but where can a man go for a quick counterfeit? Under the circumstances you, too, would have been dipping into cliché.

"Just passing by," he thundered. "Had a little time to kill. Thought I'd drop in and see how old Mac was doing. Say hello. Maybe cut up a few touches."

I had a clear enough memory of this character as I had known him in those casual encounters in the Club taproom. He had never been a loudmouth. He'd always kept his hands to himself. I was beginning to think it had to be that he was tripping and he'd hit me at the apogee of his high. If it wasn't acid or speed, I was telling myself, then this baby was a manic-depressive I had known only in his depressive phase. This time he was manic.

But he wasn't out of control. Nothing like that, brother. Actually he was in the driver's seat, and he was driving. None of that squeezing and clouting and hugging had been without method. With it he had turned me around; and once he had that arm around my shoulders, he kept it there. He was using it to keep me pointed the way he wanted me and to propel me along in this direction of his choice.

I could have dug in and stood firm. I could have pulled back toward the outer office, indicating that his touches could be cut up out there. I could even have shaken him off. I was on home ground. I had all the built-in advantages, but he was quick to forestall me.

"Your office," he whispered. "Please, Mac, your office where we can be private. Please. I know this is a crazy way to go at it, but I think you'll understand. Meanwhile the benefit of the doubt, Mac? Yes, Mac? Please?"

He was presuming. There could be no question about that. He was not presuming in quite the same way as up to then it had seemed, but he was nonetheless presuming. On what had never been anything more than the most casual contacts he was asking for special treatment. So he had a complaint or a problem. He could come with it to the DA's office quite like any other citizen and he could have the same sort of hearing as any ordinary citizen is given, and let's not be running that down any. We operate an honest office, an efficient office, and a good office and anybody who gets the routine treatment from us has nothing to complain about.

So he was pushing for special treatment; and, other than gall, I couldn't see that he had shown anything that would rate it. On the other hand, he was by no means the first citizen to approach a prosecuting attorney's office in this way. A man, for one reason or another, wants to give information to the public prosecutor. He hopes he can give information privately, without ever appearing as witness or being publicly known as an informer. Sometimes he fears for his life. More often he fears for his reputation, but either way he may be able to tell us something it will be important for us to know.

And my newly minted old buddy, Ralph Henderson, was giving every evidence of having been smitten with the privacy thing to the fullest possible degree. He seemed to have the delusion that I, an Assistant DA, could give him action all on my own, without my boss, the DA, without a grand jury, without the courts.

You're saying that's silly. So how naïve can you be? Surely you don't think that every source the DA's office has for important information must be intelligent or sensible or even sane. Kooks also come into possession of facts. Idiots talk. Imbeciles, on occasion, have made important contributions to the public welfare.

I played along with my old buddy. I ushered him into the office. Carefully—and I made my care ostentatious—I shut the door after us. I offered him a chair. I settled myself behind my desk.

"Okay, Ralph, old boy," I said, playing along with his fiction of intimacy. "What's on your mind? What can I do for you?"

I was waiting for him to begin, but he wasn't ready. First he looked the office over. He didn't go so far as to take the place apart to determine whether we had it bugged, but it was my hunch that only his ignorance of where he should have been looking for the concealed microphones and his inability to recognize one if he did see it held him back from making such a search.

What he could do, however, he did attempt.

"This is your private office?" he asked.

"As near to it as I can come," I said. "It's all the taxpayers provide."

He didn't like it. His gaze fastened on Gibby's desk. We share the office, Gibby and I. We're set up that way because so much of the time the two of us are working as a team. The rest of the reason is that we like it that way.

You may not know about me, but you certainly must know about Gibby. Officially, in our office, the office of the New York County District Attorney, Jeremiah X. Gibson is just another of us Assistant DAs. In actuality Gibby is anything but just another. Ex-cop, ex-homicide detective in the Police Department since that was the way he worked his way through college and later through law school, Gibby is the man with the nose for murder. If I have any nose at all, it is perhaps a nose for the law. Before I ever smell murder, the reek of gunpowder has to be biting my nostrils or the reek of blood has to be turning me green. Gibby has the enthusiasm. He has the ideas. He has the intuitions. I'm around to do what I can and that is mostly trying to curb his impetuosity, trying to keep him legal. Maybe I succeed, and maybe he takes care of himself. Along with his nose for murder, Gibby, I have learned, has a keen ear for the rasp of a saw. Despite my best efforts, he will go out on limbs, but he's never been sawed off. He always knows when to make the leap to safety. It can't always be an accident that his leap to safety is also invariably a leap into proof.

So now Henderson had a sour look fixed on Gibby's desk.

"You share this with somebody?" He asked.

"Another Assistant DA. He's a good guy. We work together well. I like having him around. He doesn't mind having me around."

"I do mind," Henderson said.

"And where you work you have a private office that's all your own," I told him. "But then you don't work for the taxpayers. You can get away with conspicuous waste."

He ignored the crack. Evidently he regarded it as an attempt at diversion and he had no intention of being diverted.

"No place you can go to be completely and assuredly alone with someone?" he asked.

"If someone is a girl," I said, "there are bedrooms."

"I'm not here to listen to jokes."

"I know. You were in the neighborhood and you had some time to kill, so you just dropped by to say hello. I'll go along with that. Hello, Mr. Henderson."

"If it ever gets out that I came here, it has to seem as though it was purely social. I wasn't here on business of any kind. The act I put on outside, I knew you would think I'd gone crazy, but of all the risks open to me, that seemed the best one."

"You're taking risks?" I asked.

"What do you take me for? A clown?"

"No," I said, "just something that could look like one, a man frightened out of his wits."

"A man," he said, "who can't help himself. He's forced to act, and he is frightened out of his wits, afraid he may be doing somebody a terrible wrong."

"Who's the somebody?" I asked. "I take it you are afraid for him and of yourself. You're not afraid for yourself."

"I'm afraid of myself. I'm afraid that if I do what I think I must and it should turn out that I'm wrong, that I've misjudged the whole thing, I will have done something horrible. It would be unforgivable. Certainly I would never be able to forgive myself."

"Let's explore this thing you have bugging you," I suggested. "We can do that much without getting into anything irreparable, can't we?"

I was offering openings, but he wasn't taking this one either. He was still preoccupied with Gibby's desk.

"It's his office as much as yours," he said. "He can come barging in here at any moment. He can even come in without knocking."

"He does. We never knock. No harm will ever come of it. You're ready to trust me. I vouch for him. You can trust him equally."

"I don't know him."

He was hesitating and I knew that saying it could be all he needed to bring him to a decision and that in the wrong direction. I was risking waking the man to a thought that might send him out of the office before he'd said anything. I let it slip out anyhow. I just couldn't hold it back. After all, I'm only human, if that much.

"And you know me?" I asked.

"I've been seeing you around. I'm a good judge of men."

I worked toward another opening.

"And you judge me to be a guy who on his own part might also be a good judge of men."

"You have a head on your shoulders, Mac."

"Thanks for telling me," I growled. "I'd never have known."

I was beginning to get tired of this clown.

"You see," he said in what I hoped might be the beginning of his getting down to it, "for the present at least the whole thing has to be kept unofficial. Nothing on paper. No record. Nobody but the two of us having even the remotest hint of what we're thinking."

"I'm an Assistant DA," I reminded him. "I have sworn obligations to the law."

"Right," Henderson said, "and if you need guarantees, you have them. I'm not going to ask anything of you that will in any way be a violation of your sworn obligations."

"On your interpretation of the extent of my obligation or on mine?" I asked.

"On any sensible interpretation," he said.

"And what's sensible?" I asked.

"We uncover something that's against the law," he offered. "I can't expect you to walk away from it and forget you ever knew. I can't expect you to hold still for my sweeping it under the rug."

"That's good enough," I told him. "So now what's on your mind?"

"I've come to ask a favor of you. All it will be is an hour of your time."

I looked at my watch. It wasn't one of those politely surreptitious looks. I made a show of it, hoping he'd catch the implication. He had already used up a good part of his hour and, at his current pace, he couldn't be expected to get much told within any sixty minutes.

He was bright enough. He caught it.

"This evening," he explained. "I'm asking for just an hour tonight."

"And what will I be doing?"

"Nothing," he said. "I don't want you to do a thing."

You may be thinking that wasn't much for him to be asking of me. It depends on how you read it. I could see the possibility that it might be too much. If he had been my mother, I could believe he had an idea that I'd been working too hard and that he was asking me to knock it off for just one hour that evening and give myself sixty minutes of complete rest. Since in this cloudy encounter one thing at least was clear, that he wasn't my mother, I had to look for another reading.

He had plans for this evening hour. It would be a time when he was not going to be idle and he was afraid the law would be taking an adverse view of what he intended to pull off. It did seem hardly likely that on anything so slender as our casual encounters in the Club taproom he could have come to me with the delusion that he could ask for and be granted some sort of open-ended immunity for a flouting of the law he had not yet flouted.

Any way you look at it, it was a ridiculous idea. I couldn't imagine even an old and dear friend asking that much of me. I couldn't imagine anyone being so ignorant of the way things are that he wouldn't know that such a thing would be impossible. The DA's office doesn't hand out blanket dispensations. To ask it of any single assistant in the office would be the grossest of absurdities, but then Ralph Henderson was absurd. How was I to guess the precise extent of his absurdity? I had to explore it.

"What are you going to be doing while I do nothing?" I asked.

"It's not easy to explain."

The man's discomfiture was all too obvious. He was sweating under it.

"Try," I urged.

"I don't want to say anything," he began.

"That much," I snapped, "is obvious. You've got something going and you want to drag me into it. You're not asking much, only that I go waltzing blithely into your little affair and that I go in blind. Whatever made you think you could sell me on anything that screwy?"

"Hold it, Mac." He was begging now. "Just hold it a minute. Let me try to explain. I know I sound crazy."

"And maybe you even sound devious," I growled. "Certainly presumptuous."

I had other adjectives for him, but I was holding them in reserve. Tenacious was one of them. I had reached the place where I felt I could push him hard. I was no longer afraid of losing him. What he thought he had for us could have been something or a whole lot of nothing, but it did have him bugged. Nothing I said or did was going to make him sheer off.

"I have my reasons," he said, "and you've got to believe me. They're good reasons."

"Not enough," I insisted.

"I know. I have to tell you more than that, at least let you have some idea of what my reasons are. Right at the moment I have almost nothing to go on, but tonight I'm going to try to break things open. I have to know one way or the other."

"But I don't have to know."

"You will know. That's what I'm counting on, Mac. That's why I came to you. I'm not holding out on you. You have to believe that. All I'm going on is a string of hunches and I'm not even sure they're good hunches. I don't even know whether I suspect anything. I can't even begin to put these vague suspicions of mine into words without giving them a solidity they just don't have. So don't ask me for that. I can't make wild, unfounded accusations."

"Okay," I said. "Then what can you do?"

"I don't know. That's why I need your help. I'm so confused, I don't know what to think. You won't be confused. You can set me straight. You have all the training and experience that I don't have. Also you won't have my emotional involvement. There's what I'm afraid I must believe and there is also what I simply do not want to believe. Between the two I'm whipsawed, Mac. You won't be."

"You have something you want me to look at," I said, trying to help him along. "You want me to tell you what it is. Is there actually something there or have you been seeing ghosts?"

"That's it." He jumped at my words, as though they had clarified everything and through them we had come to a complete agreement. "If I give you even the smallest hint of what's bugging me, even that can be enough to prejudice your judgment. I don't want to put any ideas into your head. I'd like you to come into this with an open mind, no preconceptions, nothing. Any conclusions you are going to draw have to be totally your own conclusions, not in any way affected by anything I've told you, unwarped by anything I may have been thinking and untouched by any of the things I've been afraid to think."

"And suppose that in my unprejudiced judgment I tell you that you have to think just what you've been afraid to think, what then? You'd better face that possibility now. I may tell you your worst fears aren't the empty phantoms you obviously want them to be."

The way he winced away from even so remote a suggestion made me feel sorry for the man. I almost wished I hadn't spoken. He pulled himself together and answered me.

"I've faced it," he said. "I had to face it before I came down here. Much as I sound like one, Mac, I'm not a fool. Of course, I'm hoping you will tell me I'm all wrong, that the signs I think I've been reading aren't signs at all, that I just wasted your time."

"Okay," I said. "That's what you hope, but you do know it's only a hope. You're not ready to admit it yet, but you do know better."

He was quick to protest that. "I don't know," he groaned, "and I must know. So tonight I'm opening it up. I'll know one way or the other."

"And when it's the way you don't want it to be? What then?"

"Then it will be in your hands," he said, dropping his voice so low that I could only barely hear him. "You'll do whatever has to be done and you'll have my full cooperation. There will be no difficulty about that, Mac. Misery, yes, but no difficulty. The way I came in here and the way I'm asking you to play along tonight, all that's on the chance that it'll go the other way. Nobody will ever know that I ever had any thoughts about it at all. It will be just between you and me that I came to you with it. I dropped by to say hello. We talked awhile about the Mets or Vietnam or anything else people talk about. It will be finished. We'll forget it, and nobody will have been hurt."

"Do you always sweat this much just talking about the Mets?" I asked.

He hauled out his handkerchief and mopped his face.

"Talking about Vietnam," he said, "I can sweat buckets."

"Then it had better be that we talked about Vietnam," I said. "Where do I go? What time do I go there? What variety of nothing do I do?"

"You will, then?"

It should have been eager and happy, but it wasn't. Maybe he'd been hoping all along that I would turn him down and he could go away and let the whole thing drop. Maybe he had just been looking for an out he could give himself. Maybe he wanted to believe his reason for doing nothing wasn't a lack of the guts it might take to push aside what he wanted to do so he could get going on what he had to do. He wanted to think he had tried to act and I had refused to cooperate. If what should have been done was going undone, he would have liked to believe it was no fault of his. Could he help it if I let him down?

"How can I unless I know where and when?" I asked.

Getting down to the specifics of time and place made him no happier, but for the time it took to give me my instructions he managed to set up between himself and his grief a screen of brisk efficiency.

He had his man coming to his office at nine. If I could manage it, I would need to be there at a quarter of. The way he wanted it, I would be witnessing the interview without taking any part in it, not even as a visible presence.

"We'll talk in my office," he explained. "There's a room opening off it. We use it as a library. There's only a thin partition and no door. If you're in there and no lights on in that library part, all you have to do is be away from the doorway—out of the direct line of sight on one side or the other. You'll hear everything that's said. Then if there's nothing to it, nobody will ever have to know I had you there."

"And if it isn't the way you hope?" I asked.

He sighed. "That way," he said, "it will be so bitter that a little more or less will make no difference."

"I come in early and you hide me away in the library to eavesdrop on your conversation."

"You're making it sound dirty," he protested.

"Sorry about that," I muttered.

He pulled himself up. "No," he amended. "You're not making it sound like anything but what it is. I know his engagements for tonight. If you come fifteen minutes before he's to turn up, there'll be no chance of your running into him. If anything, he'll be a couple of minutes late. If he leaves alone, I can watch from the window and we'll pull out after we've seen him drive away. If I have to leave with him—and I don't see how that'll be unless everything's okay and I'll have just been wasting your time—then you'll do me the favor of playing it out for me the rest of the way. You just wait in the office for me to come back and let you out. It will only take a few minutes. Or better still, when you get to the office tonight, I'll give you a set of keys. Then when we leave, you won't have to wait. You can unlock the place and let yourself out and then lock up after yourself. Whichever way, let me buy you lunch tomorrow. It can be up at the Club or down around here if that's more convenient for you. Any place you say. You name it."

I told him he could call me about that in the morning. Around the DA's office you never know. I'd have to see whether I'd be able to break loose for lunch.

He was satisfied with that. Giving me the address for his office, he made a move toward taking off. For his money we had touched on everything that needed any discussion. I waved him back to his chair.

"You've set this thing up," I said. "You know your man. I have to assume you know what you're doing; but, as you said, I have the training and experience. There may be possibilities that you are ignoring. This encounter I'm to witness. How are the chances your man will react violently?"

"You mean like throwing a punch at me?" he asked.

"Or like going for you with a letter opener. For business premises that's the standard lethal weapon."

He almost smiled, but it had too much pain in it to make it any good. I was forcing him to think about his man, to assess him as a human being, and it was obvious that such thinking opened up again that pain he had been hiding away under a layer of practical arrangements.

"In our office," he said, "nobody has that kind of letter opener. The secretaries open all the mail and they use that little machine gadget. You couldn't make a weapon of that unless you picked it up and heaved it at a man."

"Okay. How's the chances he'll be carrying a gun or even that he'll jump at your throat with his bare hands?"

"He's not that kind of guy."

"What kind is he?"

"Not that kind."

"And not the most responsive answer I've ever been handed," I said.

"I want you to judge him for yourself, but I can guarantee it.

There won't be any violence." He stopped for a moment. A thought had come up and it was troubling him. It seemed to me that he was looking for a way he could talk about it. When he spoke again, it was evident that he had found no way he particularly fancied. He was just coming out with it, letting me have it as it came without any glossing over or prettying up. "I know so little about you or about the District Attorney's office as a whole," he said. "You don't have to keep a gun on you all the time?"

"I don't have to keep a gun on me any of the time," I told him. "Mostly I don't carry one. It's only very occasional and under special circumstances."

He seemed relieved, but only because he had succeeded in getting the question out. He was less than completely satisfied by my answer.

"This isn't one of those occasions," he said. "The circumstances don't call for it. Don't bring a gun."

"I just stay snug in my hidey-hole and, if he jumps you, I wait and listen and let him take you."

"He won't even make a move that way. He's not that kind of a guy; and even if he were, it would still be all right. He'd never get to take me. I could handle him with one arm tied behind my back. Matter of fact, that's part of the reason why I want you there. It's only the smallest part, but it is a part. With you there, no matter how it comes out, I'll behave myself. I won't lay a hand on him, not even if I should want to. Without anyone around I'd like to say I could answer for myself, but I can't be sure. You'll be there. Your just being there will help me keep my head."

"But you're expecting him to keep his without any help," I said. "He's not going to know I'm right there at hand."

"That's all right. He has a head that keeps better than mine. Also he knows how we'd stack up if it came to a fight. The odds would be against him and he's not the type to buck the odds."

"Odds?" I murmured. "Ever read one of those old-fashioned gangster tales where a gun is called an equalizer?"

"Aside from the fact that as a man he just isn't right for it," Henderson said, "where would he go to get this equalizer? We don't keep guns around the office."

"He could be carrying a gun."

Henderson shrugged that off. "He doesn't," he said. "Also he hasn't a clue to why I've asked him to come in this evening. I know the man. If he had even a glimmering, it wouldn't be his way to try to handle the confrontation with a gun. Skipping the appointment altogether would be his way. He avoids confrontations. Always. Under all circumstances."

I let it rest there. "The way you talk about the man," I said, "part of the time I think you like him. Then the next minute you sound as though you have nothing for him but hate and contempt."

"Yeah," he sighed. "And pity, too. I suppose the pity hasn't been coming through to you, but that's okay. You've had enough coming through to see just how confused I am. We better not talk about it any more until after tonight. All I can do is get you confused."

I yanked open the bottom left-hand drawer of my desk. It's the one where I keep the bottle. It's not that Gibby and I spend any large part of our time in the office sloshing, or for that matter any small part of it either, but it's always a good idea to have a jug of Old Nameyourpoison handy for that odd occasion when it will come in useful.

"I'm not offering you a drink," I said. "I'm prescribing one. You'll drink it slowly. You'll relax with it. You'll get to the place where you can go out of here the way you came in. Not the way you are now, so that everyone out there will see at a glance that you've been sweating in here. You'll be casual again, breezy."

"Right," he said in a wry appraisal of his own performance. "Hail fellow all wet. I'll take your drink, Mac, and thanks for it. We'll say you've twisted my palate."

I poured him his drink and I dripped one into a glass for myself.

"To your fondest hopes," I said.

He raised his glass with mine. "And to the waste of your evening," he added.

We sipped.

"How about those Mets?" I said.

"Yeah." He played along. "And how about them Knicks?"

"Not to speak of the Kansas City Chiefs and the Republican party."

We were in the midst of that when Gibby pulled the door open and came in. He picked right up with the conversation.

"Chinese calendar," he said. "The Year of the Underdog."

I did the introductions and Gibby tilted the bottle slightly for himself. Henderson choked up, but Gibby kept the light chitchat going.

"Have you ever thought about what Lon Nol spells backward?" he asked.

Henderson didn't want to think about it. He did make a brief try at playing along while he finished his drink, but then he said firmly that he really did have to haul it. He'd already taken too much of my time.

That he had, and since from the moment Gibby came in Henderson had slipped back into that booming Big Buddy act of his, I'd had a demonstration that assured me that he was ready to bring off an exit that would be a match to his entrance. I let him go. When I returned from seeing Henderson out to the elevator, Gibby was throwing windows open. He was bringing air into the office.

"The big noise a friend of yours?" he asked.

"A guy I run into up at the Club. He dropped by to say hello."

"And that's hard work, saying hello. A man sweats so much saying hello that you can mop it off the chair he's been sitting in. You have to air the rich gymnasium reek out of the place. Show me some pieces of eight minted only last week and they'll be no more phony than your big friend. That's a man with something on his mind and it's something rough."

"He did ask me a favor."

"Let me guess. His wife—she'll be ex-Vassar daisy chain—has an innocent little hobby like cutting heroin at the kitchen sink for their kids to push in the rumpus room. So how much heft will old Mac have when it comes to calling off the Feds since just lately the Feds have been nosing around? He knows the T-men because they're the ones who wear the little American flag pins on their Timothy Leary sweatshirts."

"Baby," I said, "you're uncanny."

"Which is why the Old Man keeps us teamed up, kid. The canny Scot and the uncanny Irishman."

We left it at that. Gibby wouldn't push me. He knew that if and when I had anything to tell him, I wouldn't make him dig for it. He had a stack of paperwork to wade through and so did I. Up to the eyeballs in the paper on our respective desks, we waded, and we were still both at it when, at just a minute or two after three, my phone rang. It was Ralph Henderson again.

"Mac," he said. "I'm sorry about this morning. I moved just that little bit too fast. If I had waited only a little longer I would have known. It's all right. You can just forget about tonight. Forget that I ever came by or that I ever had a worry. It's okay."

"You're sure?"

"Of course I'm sure."

"Suppose I come around a little before nine anyway and we'll kick it around. You can tell me all about it."

"Now? When there's nothing to tell?"

"Because somebody's been leaning on you hard since you were down here, Ralph?"

"Nobody leans on me, old boy."

Maybe he was denying the suggestion and maybe he was warning me against trying it.

"So it's just that everything's cleared up and you're happy about the whole thing."

"You've hit it on the nose, old kid."

"And, of course, you wouldn't try to kid the old kid?"

"Why should I? Temporary aberration and now I'm all over it."

"Suppose I just won't be called off? Suppose I keep our appointment anyhow?"

"I won't be there. A locked office. Nobody there."

"Since you're so happy, you'll be out celebrating."

"What else?"

"I'll tell you what else. You don't sound happy. You sound worried, even a lot more worried than you were this morning when you were sweating your guts out down here. Also worried is the least of it. Now there's something more. You sound scared. You're holding your breath and you're afraid to let it go. You're praying. You're keeping your fingers crossed. You're thinking you need all the luck you can muster up. You sound desperate."

"It's the telephone," Henderson replied. "The service gets worse all the time. Even when you can get your call through, nothing sounds like what it is. You get the most extraordinary distortions. Don't tell me you haven't noticed. Everybody's complaining about it. I've heard they're combing the whole country for maintenance men to get our New York phone mess straightened out. So relax, Mac. I'm okay. It's only the way I sound and on that we'll have to wait for Ma Bell to bring us some improvement."

And that was all. With that he hung up on me. I looked over at Gibby. He had the questioning eyebrow cocked.

"Favor called off?"

"Favor called off," I said.

"He's learned they aren't the Feds. Anybody can buy those little American flag pins. They're blackmailers holed up in the last refuge of the scoundrel. He doesn't need your influence. He's paying them off."

"You're still uncanny," I said.

"And so's your loudmouth friend."

"No. He's spooky."

2

SPOOKY OR NOT, Ralph Henderson did have me spooked. I could have been telling myself that now it was a favor I didn't have to do for the guy. I was off the hook and what could be better than that? After all, working for the DA, you never have so much time off that you want to kick away even an hour of it doing favors presumptuously asked of you by a man you barely know.

I did try telling myself that, but there wasn't a word of it I could make go down. I kept remembering how Henderson had looked, how he'd sounded, and how he'd sweated. The man who dropped in on me was a man who had been going through some of the gaudier varieties of hell. He had been on to something and it had been something so grave that, whatever his wish in the matter, he just couldn't let it go by.

Now he wants me to believe that there's been a further development. He has learned he was wrong in his suspicions and this great switch is so clear and incontrovertible that everything's rosy. He doesn't need old buddy Mac.

It can't happen? Of course it can. Now that everything's cleared up, he's more than ever ashamed of the suspicions he'd been entertaining. He wants the victim of them never to know that even for a moment they had been stirring in the Henderson mind. He wants them laid away forever. He wants to forget them and he wants me to forget them. So how much will a man forget when he's been left hanging at the edge of a mystery? The nagging question—"Now what was all that about?"—it won't go away.

Certainly Henderson owed me an explanation. He could have done it without naming names. He could have kept things vague enough and general enough so that even by the most extreme stretch I could never have had a hint of the identity of the man who had been his suspect. Common courtesy would have required that he give at least that much to any man he had approached as he approached me.

In my case, moreover, there was a lot more requiring it than simple good manners. You don't go to a DA's man and open a door on to something you lead him to believe will be actionable only to turn about and slam that door in his face, leaving him to wonder just where he stands in relation to his oath of office.

Still, he had me spooked. Making that phony call, the man should have been burbling with it. He should have been pouring into that telephone a pitch of happiness that would have made the wires hum. There should have been nothing for my ear to catch but celebration and blissful relief, and I was getting none of the right sound.

There are a lot of things Gibby and I do together, including things that have nothing to do with the office. More often than not we'll eat together and on a free evening, when relaxation takes the shape of the fights at the Garden or a ball game or a show, we're likely to take our entertainments together. When either of us has a date, however, he operates as a single. We don't go in for any arrangements *à trois*, not even briefly.

That happened to be an evening when I was on my own. I had no date. I'd been thinking of lining one up, but then there had been no need since Henderson had disposed of my evening for me. A lovely Gibby's known ever since he was in shorts and she was not was cooking a steak for him, so there I was with an unplanned evening on my hands. When Gibby took off with a bottle of John Jameson under one arm and a bottle of Chateau Prieure Lichine under the other, his swap for her prime beef and lemon pie, I figured to hang on at the desk a while longer to clear away some more of the paper.

It didn't work. I could get neither Ralph Henderson nor the Henderson sound out of my head, and it took me only a few minutes of sitting there before I admitted to myself that for all the paper I was getting moved I might just as well pack it in. I pulled out of the office and headed uptown to the Club. When I'm eating alone and I'm not feeling so anti-social that I want no company but my own, the Club's the place I go. Food and drink are as good as you can want and there's always someone around to exchange the odd word with while you save one another from the stigma that attaches to solitary drinking.

You're undoubtedly having the thought that it could be someone like Ralph Henderson and doesn't that dope, Mac, ever learn? I didn't for even a moment expect it would be Henderson that evening. The Club is not a place where frightened men go. It's never been a setting for despair. I did think I might happen on someone who knew him a lot less casually than I did. I was ready to do some probing into the areas of what kind of a character he might be.

I did well for fluid and fodder and I thought I wasn't doing too badly with the probing. Many of the members knew him and all who knew him gave every evidence of liking him. From what they told me of him, he should have been quite another guy, not the man who had stopped by to see me and not the man who later telephoned. He was a gentleman. He was a solid citizen. He was the sort of guy everybody thought of as a rock in time of trouble. He was resourceful. He was unflappable. He was the take-over type but without aggression. The world was full of people who owed him. There was never a time when he wasn't doing someone a favor. He never asked a favor of anyone. People were always turning to him for advice.

A man, who might well have been the oldest living member or at least the oldest still able to stagger into the clubhouse, put it for all the rest of Henderson's friends.

"He's fatherly," the old man said. "All this psychoanalysis business is after my time. You young fellows will know better than I do what all the talk about a father image is supposed to mean, but it's what Ralph always makes me think of. I could have a son his age. Could have? Dammit, I have a grandson old enough to tread on Ralph Henderson's heels, and even to me at my age Ralph carries that feeling of authority and security. Kind, warm, dependable, generous. All that."

"What could scare him?" I asked.

"For himself nothing," the old man answered. "For you anything."

"What does that mean?"

"He has courage and he has self-confidence. I don't think he's ever been afraid of anything for himself, but he's so damn solicitous of other people, it makes a worrier of him. I don't know whether you're acquainted with my grandson, sir, but he's a good boy. Nothing wrong with him. I'm damn proud of him, but all the same I'd like it if I had one like Ralph Henderson."

It was still early when I'd finished my dinner, not quite as early as it would have been if I had been watching the time and pacing myself to keep that appointment Ralph Henderson had canceled. It was about a half hour late for that, going on to a quarter after nine. The meeting on which, before he changed his mind, he had wanted me to eavesdrop would have been going on for the better part of fifteen minutes and I couldn't get the thought of it out of my head. It was coming off as scheduled, but without me. I felt certain of that.

Henderson's office was only a short hop from the Club. I could be there in less than five minutes and maybe it was only on an impulse that I went. It would probably be nearer the truth, however, to say that all along somewhere at the back of my mind I'd had the intention lying in wait.

I went there with no settled notion of just how far I meant to carry the thing. First I was going to find out whether Henderson was there. If he should be, I would then decide on what I wanted to do next. One thing I thought I did want to do was in one way or another serve notice on the man that the Office of the District Attorney was not some mechanical convenience he could switch on and off at will.

Then, when I came to the address Henderson had given me, it was the one sort of building that had never entered into my calculations. In New York one tends to forget that not everything scrapes sky. Business can also be done in something that is neither vast nor multistoried.

The little fellows have varied histories. Sometimes they were part of the plan for their towering neighbors, a shorty sandwiched between two of the big boys to create intervening air space for the towers. Sometimes they are the property of an owner who, when the parcel for a big building was being assembled, held out for a higher price till the builders just designed around him and left him holding his little building until such time as the city's incessant reshaping of itself will bring down this big job that left him out and he has another chance in the assembling of another parcel. Sometimes it was an owner-occupied building and the owner was well suited by it. He wished to continue doing his business in it while he sat on a land value that would increase steadily under him.

Which of these histories would apply to Henderson's offices, I didn't know, but it was one of the little fellows with its neat four stories of limestone-trimmed, mellow brick sitting like a soft-voiced understatement between the glass-faced vauntings of its multilayered neighbors.

A lovingly polished brass plate fixed to the gleaming black panel of its front door said "Henderson & Crown." Evidently the offices occupied the whole building and, if there was any night watchman on duty, he would be nothing like one of those lobby guards to check on who came in and for whose offices.

All the windows were dark, but I took that to indicate only that such offices as had windows to the street were at that hour unoccupied. There would be offices at the rear of the building, and from the look of its façade it seemed very much as though even in the middle of Manhattan this was the sort of structure that would have tucked in behind it a pretty little backyard garden. And where would the senior partner—since it was Henderson & Crown and not Crown & Henderson—have his office? In front, where annoying street noises could penetrate even the best insulated windows, or at the rear, where in quiet he might look out on a patch of green, a flower bed, and perhaps an ivy-festooned brick wall?

There was a bell, a gleaming black button centering a broad circle of that same superbly polished brass I had already noticed in the name plate. I rammed my thumb down on it and I could only assume that somewhere inside it did ring. I heard nothing, but then the black-painted front door looked so thick and solid that I hadn't expected any sound to penetrate it.

I waited a couple of minutes just in case someone would come.

Nobody did. The doorknob and lock plates were brass and their polish rivaled that of the name panel and the bell. Somebody in the Henderson & Crown organization was bucking for the job of Admiral in the Queen's Navee.

Trying the knob was a reflex. I was so unprepared for its turning under my hand that I had the door swinging open before I had even registered on the startling fact that it wasn't locked. Although all along I had been considering it a strong possibility that Henderson was in the building, I had been picturing him as esconced in some office at the rear. He would be in conference and he would be neither expecting nor wanting further visitors. A ringing bell would not seriously disturb his arrangements since he would know that the ringer could not have from the street a view of any rear windows that might be lighted. He need only sit it out quietly. The would-be intruder would have no way of knowing there was anyone in the place. Having no answer to his bell, he would go away.

The same hand that polished the knob on that stout front door in all probability oiled its hinges. No door ever opened more silently. Even while it was opening under my hand I was revising my thinking. Henderson had to be there, but either there had been a revision in the time of the meeting so that it was now still about to start instead of being a half hour or so already in progress, or else the man he'd been meeting was late to the appointment or again the man had chosen not to come to the meeting.

I stepped inside and let the door shut behind me. It shut almost as silently as it had swung open, only the faintest thud as it came home into the door frame. I guessed I would be in an entrance hall, but it was all a guess. Out in the street it hadn't been glaringly light, but it was far from dark out there. There was a street light down the block. Out on the doorstep with only a little straining one could even have read a newspaper. Inside, on the other hand, it was so dark that the black of it seemed like a pressure on my eyeballs.

A hallway was the logical assumption. The totality of the darkness further indicated it. It had to be a windowless space in any event, because any window would be showing some faint glow from the street.

If there was a lighted office anywhere, it would be behind a closed door, a well-fitted door that showed no crack of light at any of its edges. Also it might have been on one of the upper floors, quite out of sight from where I stood blinking at the dark.

Feeling along the wall beside the door, my hand explored for a switch panel. I was in and that was enough. Anything further in the way of a sneaky approach gave no promise of being productive. I could see nothing in it for me unless it would be a loss of dignity and authority. In any event I was helpless in that place without light. I couldn't begin to move until I had some.

If you are looking for light switches just inside an entrance door, it ordinarily is no great area you have to cover before you come on some. There is pretty much a standard position for them, and it's only rarely that you wouldn't turn them up within inches of where you'd begun your groping.

My hand found no light switch. It found another hand. My fingers came down on it. Since the fingers had been in the act of exploring, they went on doing just that for a moment before they had even recorded a recognition of what they were touching. Convexity of knuckles, the bony articulation you can feel through the skin on the back of a hand, the short, softly bristly hairs.

I pulled my hand back. The situation, it seemed to me, explained itself so obviously that I wasn't even startled to find someone in there with me so close by that front door. I'd tried the bell. I'd had no answer. I'd heard no sounds of anyone coming to open the door for me. I'd tried the knob and come in.

Once inside, I'd heard none of my own footsteps. The floor was thickly carpeted. I could sense the luxurious feel of it through the soles of my shoes. I had been too quick by just a moment or two. My ring had not been ignored. Someone had been coming to the door. He was there with me now, reaching for the light switch. It's the natural thing to do in a dark hall before you would open the door to anyone. You switch on the light. Since he knew where it was and since he was there ahead of me, I could leave it to him to put on the lights. Muttering something like a word of apology, I pulled my hand away.

I should have skipped the apology and I should have been quicker. Even as I was withdrawing my hand, something chopped my wrist. It felt like an ax; but then, I suppose, any chop, if it is vicious enough, will feel much like any other in the dark. This one felt as though it had severed my hand. No man takes a blow like that without flaring up in an automatic resentment. He must want to fight back. You just can't have the feeling that you've been taken apart without wanting to round on your attacker to give him more than the feeling. You want to carry it all the way. You want actually to take him apart.

It was a moment in which I might have done better if I'd never been to law school. Down at the office, when the Old Man is in a good mood, he compliments Gibby on his brilliance and on the speed and accuracy of his perceptions. Me he compliments on my sound good sense, my sober and considered judgment, and on that reverence for the law that can be shaken neither by emotion or by circumstance.

So where was I in that pitch-dark hall with a chopped wrist to nurse and what was I doing? I was revering the law. I was telling myself to keep my shirt on, to make no move I would have to regret, to comport myself carefully and with full regard for my legal and constitutional situation.

Looking back on it now, I'm inclined to say that right there I did some of the quickest thinking of my career. I couldn't have had more than a splintered portion of a split second for it and I did crowd an extensive logical sequence into that immeasurably brief flick of time.

The way I assessed my position, I was the trespasser and he was on his own premises. My adversary, whether Henderson or any other legitimate occupant of the premises, could have little reason to assume that I was anything but a burglar or worse.

Nothing, therefore, could have been more reasonable than my quick decision to ignore that savage chop on the wrist. The lights would be put on. I would be recognized or, at worst, if it was not Henderson himself I had to deal with, I would identify myself and explain my conduct. There would be apologies, and they would be apologies on both sides. He would regret chopping me. I would regret frightening him.

The thinking was good enough. Show me an attorney who could do better. The intuitions, however, were wrong. No lights came on.

"Hold it, Henderson," I said. "It's M——"

I never did get my name out, but even without it I had expected that he would recognize my voice. A second chop, this one obviously aimed for my throat but not quite on target, came close enough to cut me off before I was past the initial M, and for the rest of that encounter in the dark I didn't once have breath to spare for utterance of even the shortest of words.

I was fighting for my life. At least that was what I had to believe. If the intent was to stop short of anything like a lethal conclusion, there was nothing to indicate as much.

I was tangling with this guy in the dark and he was holding nothing back. Once he had the jump on me—and don't for a moment think that the chop to my neck had missed by so much that it hadn't knocked me into a state where he had a very considerable jump on me—he could have gone for the lights and, doing better than he could in the dark, might have made short work of me.

Busy as I was with my blind efforts to fight him off, I did with some unaccountably not so busy part of me speculate about the lights.

One idea that came at me was that he didn't want to be seen. He didn't want to be recognized. He'd told me not to come. He didn't take kindly to my snooping. He was bent on teaching me a lesson, but he was aware that his reaction was excessive. I was to have my lesson but I wasn't to know at whose hands I'd taken it. So long as I didn't see him, he could pretend afterward that he hadn't even been there. He'd told me on the phone that he wasn't going to be there. Why shouldn't he pretend that I had walked in on someone he didn't even know, someone who, like me, was without any legitimate business in his offices? Blundering in there stupidly, I had interrupted a burglar at his work. I had no one to blame but myself.

That idea came and it went. Some moments later, after three glancing and peculiarly light punches to my head and one on-target and savagely heavy kick to my groin, it returned but in a different guise. Maybe this was it. I wasn't tangled with Henderson at all. This was some crook who had been before me in the breaking and entering.

If at that point I could have stopped thinking and let a complete absorption with the punching and wrestling erase everything else for me, I might have been the better for it.

We were getting nowhere. The best I could manage was holding him off, dodging enough to keep his blows from landing squarely and trying not to think that sooner or later accident would do for him what so far his best efforts had failed of accomplishing. It seemed inevitable that one of these times I would dodge the wrong way or in an ill-chosen rhythm I would run the point of my chin squarely into his fist.

It was hard to keep track of directions in the dark, but we hadn't been playing this game for more than three or four turns before I was convinced that at least this much I had figured soundly. There was one particular corner where he wanted me. Persistently and with the greatest concentration he was trying to work me over there. Blow by blow and turn by turn I had less and less with which to fight him off. I never did recover from the jump he had taken over me at the start and, with every kick or chop he landed, he increased his advantage over me. He was chopping me down bit by bit. I was managing nothing more than fending off the finalizer.

It was only a flick of his fist to my nose, but combined with a slicing kick that followed right after it to catch me square on the ankle, it was enough. I was going and I knew it. He had me backed off and I couldn't slip into another turn. He was riding me back. I was headed for the spot he had for some reason picked for his killing ground.

From the first I had known that only by a miraculous stroke of luck could I ever overcome his initial advantage sufficiently to give me any hope of taking him. Quickly I recognized that it wasn't my night to get lucky.

I could see only one small chance. It was thin but I had to grab at it. If I could only keep the struggle going long enough, some help for me might walk in that front door. He had been here waiting in the dark behind that unlocked door. He couldn't have been waiting for me. I hadn't been expected, but he had been waiting for someone. It could be that he knew I wasn't his man. Even the few words I'd managed before he silenced me might have told him that much. All it needed was that he knew the voice of the man he'd been waiting to ambush.

I rather thought that he didn't know. Certainly, if he had known, he wouldn't have taken the time for all this fancy footwork. He would have put the whole of his weight behind his punches and disposed of me as quickly as possible. His man was still to arrive and he'd have to be an idiot to risk being tied up with me when the man he'd been waiting for would come in through that front door.

If this notion hadn't been kicking around in my head, at first half formed and then fully, I might have made some further tries at talking to him. There were moments when I could have managed to gasp out the odd word or two, but there was that one chance I saw for myself and I wasn't going to spoil it. Let him think he had his man. Let him have his fun. If the fun could be prolonged sufficiently for him to be surprised by a second visitor coming through that unlocked door, that could be it. Could be? It would be. It had to be.

This caller could hardly be a friend of his. I could look for the second man to come into an alliance with me. I just had to keep the fight going long enough. I couldn't believe that the reserves wouldn't be coming up. The U.S. Cavalry had to be riding to the rescue. The bugles would sound the charge. The troops would come surging through that unlocked door. What other end could the story have? Didn't they always end that way?

Maybe they did but not for a dazed and dizzied DA's boy who had slipped so far that he let himself forget that he was fighting on ground he didn't know against an enemy who all too obviously did know it. I was reminded, but by then it was too late.

My opponent's heavy rush carried me back and I could neither hold against it nor circle away out of it. I began hoping for the solid wall that would come up against my back. This space we were in couldn't be limitless.

If I could be ready for it the moment my back touched against it, there was the chance that he wouldn't succeed in pinning me to it. If I could be quick enough, I just might manage to use it as a push-off point, letting it bounce me into the offensive rush I was too chopped down to mount without it.

There was no wall, or anyhow I didn't reach it. I did back into something. It took me just at ankle height and it wiped my feet out from under me. I went down hard; and, when I hit, I smacked against a floor that seemed to be no place it should have been. It was a lot higher than it had any right to be.

I'd been flattened and yet I hadn't been. How can a man be flattened if he hasn't a flat floor under him? Under me I had a bewildering range of levels and the edge of each level bit into me when I hit. Even if I'd had any bounce left in me, which I didn't, I couldn't possibly have bounced back out of that decking. Whatever it was that was under me was too disorienting. It offered me nothing I could rely on.

Anyhow there wouldn't have been the time. Immediately after I went down, the blow fell. It crashed against my skull and shattered into what seemed like a million pieces.

3

Coming back out of unconsciousness is at best a confusing trip. Coming back alone and in the dark is confusion further compounded. It is almost as though even the classic question—"Where am I?"—doesn't apply. What you are more likely to be asking is "Am I anywhere?"

Unable to see, you make muzzy stabs at concentrating on your other senses. You listen hard, but all you can hear is the pulse of the blood inside your aching head and the rasping of your breath in your throat. You try to feel, but there you discover that you're equally limited. Most of your comeback seems to be in the form of rapidly growing awareness of a great variety of pains, aches, and strains, but you quickly have come to know all you want to know about those.

You need a little outside information. You'd like to know where you are and what it is you're lying on. It seems most peculiar that you should be lying the way you are. You would expect to be flat on your back, but you aren't. You're not flat and you're lying on your side. Lying on your side with your arms behind you? That puts one of your arms most uncomfortably under you and the other one pulling so hard on your shoulder socket that it won't take much more to have you unhinged.

So you'll change that. You'll bring your arms forward. The one you have under you feels as though your body weight pressing it hard against some crazy ridges you're lying on will break it in at least two or three places. The strain on the other arm is growing steadily more painful. Even while you're thinking of bringing your arms forward, however, it comes to you that it's exactly what you've been trying to do even before you'd consciously thought about it. At least part of your feeling of imminent shoulder dislocation has been coming from your straining to move your arms into a more comfortable position. You can't bring them forward. They won't come.

I was lying there tied at wrist and ankle. My hands were bound behind my back, but that wasn't the whole of it. In addition to being tied together, both the wrists and the ankles were tied to something.

By pressing my wrists hard against the thing they had between them I could get enough feel of it to establish for myself some of its characteristics. It was immovable. Even when I put all the strength I could muster into the effort, I couldn't shake it. It was a solidly fixed vertical post, probably of wood. Since whatever my ankles were feeling was somewhat masked by my socks, they were telling me less than I could learn from my bare wrists, but there was nothing to indicate that what I had down there was in any respect different from the thing I felt between my wrists.

I was lying at a slant with my head much higher than my feet. All the way up and down my body I had this evenly spaced series of sharp edges to bite into my flesh. The posts were vertical. The edges were horizontal and the line of the posts were perpendicular to the direction of the edges. My head ached both inside and out and there was something most peculiarly wrong with my mouth, but I was leaving that part of me for thinking about later. The picture I had clicking into shape had to do with only all of the rest of me, my body from the shoulders on down.

I was tied hand and foot to a pair of posts. In the vertical axis these posts were parallel. Horizontally they were at different levels and the level of each corresponded to a ridge I had under me. I wasn't tied down to the floor. I was tied down to a flight of stairs, bound hand and foot to the posts of the stair rail.

Up to that point I had been straining forward, trying to pull away. Now, edging myself back, I had quick verification. I could feel all the intervening posts of the stair rail, one for each step I felt under me. So then memory came at me with further verification. I'd had that hunch that my adversary had been trying to work me around to some specific spot, a precise place he had chosen for bringing me down. I remembered his maneuverings and I also remembered that when I had gone down, it had been as much by virtue of something that took me at ankle level and cut my feet out from under me as through the blow he had simultaneously landed.

While all these thoughts were going through my head, I was otherwise busy. Only the first of it had been instantaneous, the realization that I was tied down and on what and to what. Everything that followed, the remembering and the search for explanations, was just something to keep my mind going while my body worked at trying to free my wrists and ankles. Pain or no pain, I was straining at my bonds, tugging at them hard, trying to break them.

The process involved getting as much of my body weight into it as my awkward position would allow. It involved bounding hard against the steps and every bounce was murderously bruising, not to speak of what those bounces were doing to my arms and shoulders. Past the pain of it, however, I found that my thrashing about on the steps brought me an unlooked-for satisfaction.

It was only in hearing my thumps and thuds that I first realized how heavily I'd been oppressed by the total dark and the complete silence. I was, at least, making some sort of sound. It was a break through that totality of nothingness in which I'd been enveloped.

Perhaps if I had just lain there and been quiet, I might have heard him move through the hall. I don't know. It was just as likely that I would have heard nothing. What could have been quieter than the way the door had opened under my hand or what more silent than the way I had come into the place. He had been there then and he had moved to chop my wrist and I'd heard nothing.

It's a useless speculation. In any event the first I knew that there was anybody still about was when in the midst of my pounding myself against the stairs I saw the dim light filter briefly in from the street. The front door had opened and as quickly been shut again. Without even stopping to think whether what I was doing was wise or stupid, I tried to shout. There could have been someone out there, some passer-by I could reach with a cry for help. I tried, and nothing came.

So then I knew what I might have known earlier, had I given it any thought. I was not only bound. I was gagged as well. That was what was wrong with the way my mouth felt. Now that I knew it, I could feel against my tongue and lips the texture of the gag. I was also getting the taste of it.

I gave up on trying to shout and worked at making what noise I could. I pounded my body against the stairs. I bucked backward to slam hard against the posts of the stair rail. I discovered that what had seemed moments before a comforting noise was now exasperating. Tied as I was, I could bring neither fists nor heels into play.

I was beating myself up and I was achieving nothing but a series of muffled thumps. What I was striking against was certainly hard enough, but I had nothing with which to pound on it but the softest parts of my body.

Meanwhile there were other sounds and they were far louder than the best I could achieve. They came from the direction of the once more closed front door. I heard the rasp of metal as it slid against metal. I heard the solid bang of metal rammed against metal. For a moment I lay still and listened, and within that moment it was over. It was back to what it had been before, total silence re-established in the total dark.

I had no way of knowing that I was now alone, but every instinct was telling me as much and quickly reason came marching up in support of instinct. The man had knocked me out. It had been a good knockout, running well past any ten-count, but even a good knockout will give you no more than a few minutes before consciousness begins seeping back in. Anything much longer falls into another department. It takes on the dimensions of coma. It involves at least a mild concussion and I had in my time been through that sort of thing. I had a good memory of how it feels when you come out of anything that traumatic.

Just from the way I was feeling I knew I hadn't been out for long. It had to be that it was only long enough for him to have bound me hand and foot and secured the gag. I could guess that I'd returned to consciousness immediately after he had finished with me or so very short a time thereafter that it made no difference.

That I'd also had time enough for pulling myself together, coming to a clear picture of my situation and even on making a start toward trying to do something about it before I'd seen that light come in from the street indicated that my man had not been in quite as much a hurry to separate himself from the scene as might have been expected.

Perhaps he had lingered till he could hear me make an effort to free myself and by listening assure himself that he had done a good enough job and that I would hold. That was one possibility. Another was that when I rang the bell, I had interrupted him at something he'd been doing in those offices. Having disposed of me and secured me, he had, before taking off, gone back and cleared away all unfinished business.

Anyway I looked at it, the man had taken off. I was now alone. I could imagine no other possibility. I wriggled around for a while trying for a position that might be easier than anything I had thus far managed. The best I could do took some of the pull off my shoulders, but nothing would cushion the edges of the steps and up and down the full length of me where each of the rises met its tread there was the corner to bite into me.

If he had left me secured to some more endurable surface, I might have taken the easier way. I might even have tried to sleep. However I dealt with it, I wasn't going to be there forever. Morning would come and, with morning, an office staff. It was a midweek night. There was a working day coming up. With my wrists tied behind me I couldn't bring my watch around to any place where I could get a look at its luminous dial, but making guesses at the time, I had to settle for something not too much after ten o'clock. If Henderson & Crown ran a nine-o'clock office, it would be eleven hours to wait on those stairs.

Thinking about eleven hours, I couldn't make it seem anything less than an eternity. I was getting nowhere with my thrashing about. I tried it another way. Slowly and silently I hauled at my bonds, exerting on them the hardest pull I could muster and listening carefully. I had myself fully alerted to catch even the slightest crepitation that might come to my ears or to recognize the feel of even the slightest yielding in the fabric of whatever it was that he had used for binding me up. I heard not the faintest sound of ripping. I felt nothing yield.

I allowed myself a minute or two of rest. There was all too little I could learn of the precise dimensions of the fix I was in, but I was telling myself that even the smallest scraps of knowledge might be of some help to me. I did a mental exploration of my whole body, trying to separate out all my discomforts so that I might think about each of them individually, trying to read out of them whatever they could tell me about the details of my predicament.

My pains and discomforts just about explained themselves. Oddly, however, in the course of my stock-taking I found that I also had a couple of comforts and it was those that needed thinking about. Everybody knows the standard things to do for a man who has passed out. You loosen the man's tie and open his collar to free him of any constriction around the throat. You also unbuckle his belt. Doing these little things for him may be beneficial. They are certain to make him more comfortable.

Ducking my head, I could feel with my chin. I felt neither tie nor shirt. I felt the skin of my chest. Turning my head from side to side with my chin still ducked down, I did feel the cotton of my shirt. I even felt a fuzzy edge and I took it to mean that my collar had ripped open. That much was understandable. The man who had trussed me up on those stairs had obviously not loosened my tie and unbuttoned my collar. What interest he'd had in me had not lain in the direction of seeing to my comfort or my welfare. Also, if there had been a loosened tie, I could have found it with my exploring chin. I had no tie hanging around my neck.

He had also removed my belt. I was just that touch looser around the waist, and that made a second thing he had done and not for my comfort. It figured. Tie and belt—he had taken them off me and he had used them for binding me up. One would be on my wrists and the other on my ankles.

For only a couple of moments I lay there wishing there were some way I could know which he had used for which. From neither belt nor tie was it going to be easy to break loose, but if I could choose between the two, the silk of the tie could be expected to give long before I would be making much more than a dent in that unnecessarily stout cowhide I'd been using for holding my pants up.

I did allow myself the futility of wishing I might have been the sort of slob who has never given a thought to the quality of the stuff he wears. I was stricken with sharp pangs of longing for a sleazy tie and a cheap belt, one of those fake-leather jobs that wouldn't stand up to even a week of ordinary wear.

Even while I was indulging myself in such wishfulness, I started working on things as they were. I had no choice. Whichever it was that he had used for binding my wrists, that was the thing I had to work at breaking. If I could only achieve the use of my hands, the rest would be easy.

Exploring for better methods, I discovered that by working knee and shoulder against the steps I could win me some three or four inches of movement up and down. With this movement the bond that held my wrists slid against the post. When I held it taut during this sliding movement I felt in it a succession of catches and releases. I tried to get my hands around to feel of the post, but the way they were secured I couldn't make it. It didn't matter. I knew I wasn't dealing with slickly streamlined posts. Whether they were turned or carved or both mattered little. They were ornamented and the ornamentation afforded me some sort of an abrasive surface I could work against. I couldn't hope it would be anything as useful as a sawtooth edge, but it was something. It was my best hope.

I ran through my limited range of possible movements and positions, trying for the angle that would give me the maximum pull and the heaviest friction. I found I had little choice. Each different angle I attempted began as an acute discomfort and swiftly grew into an agony. I worked from each in turn as long as

I could whip myself into taking it and then I would change, not because I was kidding myself that one was better than another but only because when one part of me had been strained and battered beyond the limits of endurance it did help to shift both strain and battering to some other part of my body.

I made myself promises. I wasn't going to allow myself even a moment's rest. There would be such little changes of position as I could manage, but there would be no other easement. There was to be no intermission in my sawing until, one way or another, I would be set free.

I did try to keep these promises and for long periods of time I kept them well. Eventually, however, exhaustion caught up with me, and it was true exhaustion. I not only rested. I even slept. I didn't sleep much and it wasn't sustained sleep. It was just a succession of little naps, and each time I woke from one I hated myself for it. Don't ask me whether I was hating myself for the weakness that let me doze off or for the strength that persisted in bringing me back out of sleep for yet another bout with my discomforts and my agonies.

I settled into a pattern over which I had less and less control. I worked and I slept. I worked and I slept.

How much quicker it might have been if I could have kept at it without the intervening naps I don't know, but it was a long time. I had fallen into one of my exhausted little sleeps and, coming out of it and forcing myself back to the endless and hopeless sawing, I had what seemed nothing less than a miracle. At the very first rub against the post, I felt it and I heard it. It was like a stuttering whisper, the sound of ripping silk.

Obviously it had begun some time near the end of the previous bout of sawing when I'd been too exhausted to notice the beginnings; for once it started, it went quickly. Since I now had the thing weakened and had to some extent frayed it out, I now returned to my first method. Disregarding all bruises and strains, I gathered myself for a violent lunge away from the balustrade. One lunge didn't do it. It took several, but on each the weakened fabric gave a little more and just as it had come to feel as though the next attempt would slice my hands off, they finally did break loose and it wasn't my hands that gave. I had them freed.

Immediately I sent them into action. They were numb from having been bound so long, but their first task was an easy one. Even numb fingers could handle removal of my gag since they weren't too numb to recognize the feel of Scotch tape. The gagging had been a simple and efficient job. A wad of linen had been stuffed into my mouth and secured there by a criss-cross of Scotch tape that ran from right jaw to left cheek and from right cheek to left jaw. Once I'd ripped away the tape, the gag came bulging out between my lips. I'd been gagged with my own handkerchief.

At first touch down around my feet my fingers found the belt buckle. Immediately they had it opened. I was in great shape. I had restored to myself the use of all my limbs. I made a try at scrambling to my feet. It wasn't even a good try. They had more numbness in them than my hands. All that sawing had kept the circulation going through my arms and the muscles there were limber. My leg muscles were not. They needed a little time to make their comeback.

They buckled under me. I fell down the stairs, but that sounds worse than it was. I'd been tied pretty much at the foot of the flight. I didn't have far to fall. Maybe I did pick up a bruise or two when I hit, but by then I had so many so well distributed over my legs and side and back that it is more likely that I only aggravated a few of the earlier accessions.

Standing was going to have to wait a little. Locating the bottom step, I pulled my butt up on it and for a minute or two I sat there quietly and massaged my calves and ankles. My eye caught the gleam of the luminous dial of my wrist watch. I could read it clearly. The hands had crept some minutes past midnight. I wasn't surprised. If I'd had to guess it, I'd have said I'd been tied to that stair rail even longer.

While I was waiting for my legs to come around, I made a few simple plans ahead. Once I was again on my feet, I'd find myself the light switch and get myself out of there. Once I'd gone even that little way with my thinking, it occurred to me that I didn't have to wait for the light switch. Even sitting there on the step I could have a little light. There was my cigarette lighter.

Reaching for it in my pocket where I always carry it, I came up empty. My fingers came on all manner of useless things I carry in the same pocket, but no lighter. I did the exploratory tour of all my pockets. The lighter hadn't strayed. It was gone.

It was obvious that I had been robbed. Sitting on the step in the dark, I did the best inventory I could manage under the circumstances. My watch was still with me. I'd just checked the time on it. I still had a pocketful of change and I still had my billfold.

But then what kind of a robbery is it that takes nothing but an ordinary, inexpensive cigarette lighter and two or three folders of throw-away paper matches while it is passing up a good watch and even a few bucks of the negotiable? I left thinking about that one for later.

Meanwhile I was to have no immediate light, not even some small gleam of it unless you want to count the face of my watch. My first moves were going to have to be made on grope and hope with possibly some small assist from the power of thought.

I was sitting on the bottom step of a flight of stairs. When my legs would be ready for it, I would feel my way to a wall and then follow along till I'd feel under my hands the wood paneling of the front door. Alongside that door I'd find the light switches. I knew where they had to be. Only that first chop at my wrist had kept me from finding them at the beginning.

But at that stage of things, you must be asking what would I want with lights? Why not just open the door and get myself out of there?

May I suggest that this would be layman's thinking. I was doing DA's office thinking. I knew exactly where I was. I was at the scene of a crime.

Any first thoughts I might have had under which I stood in the role of the uninvited invader confronted by a legitimate occupant risen to the defense of his property and person had been difficult to sustain even through the course of our hand-to-hand struggle. There was something too peculiar about the man's fighting methods. I hadn't understood them then and even at this later time while I was sitting on that step and pulling myself together I still couldn't understand them.

What his later acts had clarified, however, went in the direction of establishing him as a person who had been on the premises for no legitimate purposes. The fact that he had persisted in keeping me in that total darkness even after he had knocked me out and secured me to the stair rail certainly indicated that he knew that his activities couldn't stand even the light of an electric bulb.

A non-criminal adversary might have tied me up just to have me secured for as long as it took him to call the police. He would have had no need for gagging me and none for depriving me of my cigarette lighter and matches. Also in securing and gagging me he would have had no need for being so careful to use nothing that could be traced to anyone but myself.

If all that isn't enough to establish the man as someone who stood on the wrong side of the law, I submit to you the hours that had gone by since he had subdued me. I've heard all the outraged tales about how long you may have to wait for the police when you need them, but even the most exaggerated of these complaints never stretches the waiting time to hours.

It couldn't have been clearer. I had a crime to report. In my capacity as one of the assistants in the DA's office I had a crime to investigate. That was what I was thinking while I sat on that step getting myself pulled together. I was going to find the lights and then I was going to find the telephone. I had no interest in getting away from there. I would call the police and, while waiting for them to turn up, I could make a start on looking around the premises in an effort to determine the nature of whatever crime it may have been that my visit had interrupted.

I pulled myself up off the step and shuffled forward, testing the footing and holding my hands out in front of me seeking out that street door which had to be straight ahead of me. My fingers touched and it was exactly as I had expected. I could feel the door panels and their framing moldings. Exploring to my right, I came on the cooler feel of metal, the brass of the lock plates and then the smooth bulk of the doorknob fitted to my hand.

That completed my orientation. I knew precisely where my hand would come on the light switch. What it found was a battery of switches, and I flipped the lot, running my hand along the whole row and hitting each in turn, and I was still standing in total darkness.

I thought of a blackout, but I kicked the thought away. A general blackout occurring simultaneously with my personal one was too unbelievable a coincidence. This light failure was again something that could be called all my own. It was an extension of my loss of cigarette lighter and matches. My assailant had snatched the light bulbs as well.

It was a setback but I didn't think it would be serious. I could grope my way along the walls till I'd hit the first office door. It hardly seemed likely that he would have blacked out the whole building.

I found an office door, and when I opened it I did have light. It wasn't much, but the office had windows to the street and through those windows filtered enough glow from the street lights to permit me to make out shapes. I located a desk and a desk chair, a couple of chairs for visitors, what seemed to be the usual filing cabinets and such. I also located the desk lamp.

The wall switch in the office had done me no more good than had the ones out in the hall. Flipping that one had also turned on nothing. I tried the desk lamp and did no better with that. Feeling my way up the shaft of the thing, I closed my hand over the bulb. It was there.

It was no good doing any further fumbling around the building to try other offices. In taking care of the lights he had obviously gone to the source. He had located the fuse box and pulled the fuses. I could assume that he'd pulled all of them. I was beginning to think he would have doused the street lights as well if he could have managed it. The guy was thorough.

Since the glow that filtered in from the street was enough for locating the desk lamp, I needed only to put my mind to it to make out the other shapes of desk furniture. There was only one item I wanted and I quickly found that. It was the one thing I did need, the telephone. I picked it up and waited for the dial tone. Dialing would be no problem. The police emergency number I could do by braille.

I got no dial tone. I didn't even get any static. I knew at once that my man had taken care of the phone just as he had taken care of the lights, but I told myself that the situation was building to dimensions that seemed far too extreme. Why had he gone to so much trouble, doing all this with the lights and the telephone? It was excessive. It could serve no possible purpose. But I mustn't jump to conclusions.

4

Pulling on the telephone cord, I came up against no resistance and, playing it through my hands, I soon came to the end of it. I wanted to think it was on a jack and had merely pulled out, but my fingers told me different. The cord had been cut. Either this was an operation I hadn't even begun to understand or the guy had to be some kind of a nut who carried everything to excess.

I thought of groping my way into some of the other offices on the chance that he hadn't done them all, but I told myself it would be a waste of time. It would make no sense for him to do one telephone and leave me the others. Although I did recognize that all these excessive measures for cutting me off from light and communication were making no conceivable sense to me, I felt that for the man to have gone to such extremes without making them complete would be much too insane.

I had gone far enough with this fumbling around in the dark and the semidark. I didn't have to be inflexible about it. The situation called for nothing more than a small change in procedure. I would do what any layman might have done. He would have done it in the first place. It wasn't difficult to find my way back the way I had come. I now knew the distances. I knew I could go the whole route back to the street door and not stumble over any obstructions. I'd get myself out of the place, find me the nearest pay phone, make my police call, and then return and wait for the boys to come along.

By then, I suppose, I should have known better. Reaching the street door was as easy as I'd expected, but that was as far as I went. It was solidly locked. I could turn the doorknob but that was all I could do with it. There were a couple of other locks on that door and they offered to my exploring fingertips nothing but keyholes. They had been locked with keys, and without keys they couldn't be unlocked.

Expanding dimensions? Can you see what that locked door was now telling me about my man? The lighter, the matches, the lights, the telephone, and the locking of the street door had all been designed to keep me out of action for all that remained of the night. When he left the building, he still had work to do. If he couldn't keep me incommunicado for the whole of the night, I was going to be able to forestall whatever it was that he'd been planning to do during the succeeding hours.

I could make no specific guess of what the man's plans might have been or even of what he thought I could have done to forestall him, but I could figure a possibility. I'd work myself loose. I'd get the word to the police. Whether I got in touch with Henderson or they did wouldn't matter. Henderson would almost certainly know who the man was and he was very likely to know what the man would be doing. After all, I did have that much history on the thing. Henderson had come to me with suspicions.

Later he called me off with that all too lame business about finding that his suspicions had been groundless. That I hadn't believed from the first, but even if Henderson had been snowed into a sense of false security, it would take more than an avalanche-sized snow job to stand up in the face of what had happened to me in the Henderson & Crown offices that night. It could even be that my man's plans called for getting himself out of the country before I would have any possibility of putting myself back in touch with the outside world.

And this was another thing I knew about my man. He had keys to the building, and they weren't any spare set an ordinary burglar might have picked out of a desk drawer in one of the offices. People who have locks like that don't close their offices for the night and go off without locking the door. This had to be somebody who had used his keys to come into the building. Expecting no interruptions and thinking he would do what he had to do there quickly and be quickly away, he hadn't slowed himself up by stopping to lock the door after himself as he came into the building. He was just going to pop in and pop out again and he was in a hurry.

The whole thing was fitting together and it was telling me something more about the man. It was more important to him that I remain incommunicado for as long as possible than for him to try to conceal the fact that he was a man who had keys to the building.

It occurred to me that this would hardly be the only door. Somewhere there would be a fire door, but that was only a thought. It was too obvious that there could be a dozen doors and no possibility that any of them would do me a bit of good.

I thought I had available to me a far better bet. There were windows. I had just been in a room that had windows and those windows looked out on the street. It was, furthermore, a ground-floor room. It would be no trick at all to go out by one of those windows. My man might be kidding himself that he'd thought of everything or he might have just settled for doing everything he could and hoping I wouldn't think of the windows, but it made no difference. I headed back to that office I had just left and I didn't have to go even a step beyond its doorway before I knew that my imprisonment had been set up for me by a man who missed out on nothing.

I wasn't going out through any ground-floor office window. They were barred. How I missed that the first time I was in there is easily understood. This is a New York fact of life. If you have ground-floor windows you have bars on them. Our burglary rate runs too high for anything else. Those wrought-iron bars on ground-floor windows are so much a commonplace that you see them without taking any notice of them.

Now, however, I was taking notice of them and with them I was now registering something else to which I had previously given no attention. Out in the darkness of the front hall I had known that there were stairs, but I'd known it only because I had been bound down to them. How long a flight it might be that led up to the second story of Henderson & Crown offices I'd had no way of knowing. Even in this office, where I had the benefit of such street lights as filtered in, it wasn't enough to allow me to make any direct estimate of ceiling height, but, now that I was thinking about it, I did see that I had an index.

The faintly grayed rectangles that were the windows were discouragingly tall. I could expect that the upstairs windows would not be barred, but I could also expect that the distance from second-floor window ledge to street would be too great for any reasonable possibility of a safe drop down to the pavement. It was discouraging, but I told myself I had no choice but to explore it.

Returning to the hall, I felt my way back to the stairs. Guiding on the stair rail, I galloped up the stairs in the dark. On the second floor I felt my way along the walls in search of another office door. Quite accidentally my hand encountered a light switch. With no expectations I flipped it and it was as expected. He had killed this light as well as the ones downstairs. Although I planned to try every light switch I might happen upon, I wasn't going to make any search for them. It was too likely that he hadn't stopped to be selective. He had cleared the whole fuse box.

I found the door I wanted and beyond it another office. Here I was a little better off for light than I'd been in the office downstairs. This one had its windows nearer the level of the street light. The glow that came in was brighter. Easily I located the various pieces of office furniture. On the desk I could see a telephone clearly silhouetted against the window glow. I had to pass the desk on my way to the window. I tried the telephone as I went by. It was, of course, as dead as the one down below and also, like that one, it was trailing a severed cord.

I didn't stop to mourn it. I was definitely down to the windows. It would be all or nothing there, and even before I came close enough to touch them I saw it was going to be nothing. Despite all its elegances of another day, the building had been provided with all the modern mechanical amenities. Air-conditioned, it had no openable windows. The plate glass was sealed in.

Ever notice how you can go along and not be even remotely aware of something and then, when you do become aware of it, it will suddenly become overwhelming? It was only when I was trying to open those windows and couldn't that I had even the first awareness of the place being stuffy. Of course, with all its ventilation provided by the air-conditioning system and the electric power off for hours, it would have to be stuffy in there; but, unnoticing as I had been earlier, now that I knew there was no fresh air coming in and, more than that, even the stale enclosed air not circulating, I suddenly felt as though I were suffocating.

I felt of the window glass and, peering through it to the street, I made estimates on how high up I was. I played with the idea of picking up the telephone and using it to crash out the glass. It could, of course, be done; but then what? I would have a window with a murderously jagged hole in it.

I gave up on the unbarred windows. What little I might manage to do for myself would be better done downstairs. I went back to the lower floor. By this time I was an old hand at negotiating the pitch-black hall. Frustrated as I was, I got a disproportionate thrill of satisfaction from the ease with which I made my return to the first office I had tried. When an ego has been as much flattened as mine then was, even so minute a show of competence can be enough to give it a lift. I knew what I was going to do and just how I would go about doing it.

I headed straight for one of the barred windows and on my way past the desk I picked the telephone off it, carrying the instrument with me to the window. Holding the telephone poised, I waited. You must remember that in Manhattan's business districts just those streets that are most traffic-choked by day come closest to being totally devoid of life during the night.

This was such a street. It had nothing along it but offices and businesses that would cater only to the office workers. I could see the dark fronts of lunchrooms and sandwich shops. Directly across the street I could make out the signs of a paperback bookstore and a unisex boutique, but their windows were also dark.

Anything that would pass this way would only be rolling through, but it couldn't be that I would have any long wait before something did come rolling through. Even in its closed-down hours any Manhattan street remains in almost continuous use at least as a means of getting from one place where the action is to some other.

After a few minutes of waiting I did see a car come into the street. I hefted the telephone and waited. Just a moment before the car would be abreast of my window I moved. Whamming the phone against the window, I crashed the glass. I wanted a loud noise and I got one. It was beautiful, like an explosion, and it didn't go unheard. The driver of the passing car rammed his foot on the gas and zoomed through so fast that I wondered how he'd managed to leave no jet trail hanging in the air under the street lights.

I shouted after him.

I yelled: "Help!"

I yelled: "Police!"

I had no way of knowing whether I was heard or not. I worked at not being too discouraged. So a coward was driving that car. He'd had no thought but getting his own hide safely away from the vicinity. It was all right. I hadn't been asking for heroism. What was to say that, once he was out of the street, he wouldn't go looking for the nearest phone booth? Even while I was thinking about it, he might already be passing the information on to the police. I told myself it was all right. I told myself it was precisely the way a prudent citizen would handle the situation. I didn't convince myself.

I stood by the broken window waiting and watching. Even at that hour luck might bring me a passing pedestrian. Even if at my first shout he would take to his heels, the nimblest-footed of men could hardly take himself out of earshot before I would have time for a few words of explanation and reassurance. I might even find some convincing words. I might even be believed. I wasn't asking for much, only that someone make that quick call that would bring me the police.

That lucky I wasn't. No pedestrians came my way. Cars did come whizzing through the street. I would shout at them, but I could see nothing in their passage to indicate I'd even been heard. Nobody slowed down, and nobody accelerated. They all came flying through. Mere shouting would obviously never be enough. I took to flailing at the remains of the shattered window with the useless telephone I still had in my hand, adding the crash of breaking glass to whatever I could achieve in the way of yelling.

Making a fresh assault on that window each time another car hit the street, I was rapidly approaching the place where I would be running out of window glass. Just before I might have been forced to move along and start on another window, I got what I had been waiting for. A car turned into the street and, as it approached, it slowed. I flailed away at the remnants of glass that still hung in the window frame and I gave out with everything my lungs had in them.

As it pulled up closer, I recognized it. It was a police patrol car. The boys had finally made the scene. I set the telephone aside. As I turned back to the window, the glare of a flashlight hit me full in the eyes. Just on the reflex I dodged away from it.

"Hold it right there," the cop with the flashlight ordered.

I couldn't conceive of a more superfluous order.

"No place for me to go," I said. "You're going to have to get me out of here."

"Now, none of that," he snapped. "You're coming out, and now."

"Suppose you tell me how I do that," I snarled.

I'd had all the hard time I was prepared to take in any one night. I was in no mood for taking it from the police.

"The way you went in," the cop said. "You smashed the window and climbed in. It's still smashed. You can climb out."

"Between the bars?"

The officer looked at the bars. They gave him no pause.

"I don't know how you squeezed through, but if you could do it to get in, you can do it coming out and this I want to see."

It was a stupid colloquy and, much as this cop was irritating me, I forced myself to the recognition that it was more my fault than his. I'd been asking him to come up with some sort of a miracle of instant comprehension. I had no right to expect it and meanwhile time, which I had steadily been coming to feel was more and more of the essence, was wasting. I tried another tack.

Stupidly I made my first move toward it by reaching into my pocket for my identification.

"None of that," my cop growled. "I've got my gun on you along with my light. Come away from your pockets."

I came away from them. "Sorry," I muttered. "As soon as I've identified myself we can start making sense. All I was reaching for was my identification."

He indicated that for the moment he could do without it. All he was requiring of me was that I should squeeze my way out between the bars. He was prepared to stack me up against the hood of the prowl car and frisk me. If I had any identification on me, I could leave that to him. He would find it.

"I didn't break in," I insisted. "I've been trying to break out. I came in by the door."

"Okay. Hold it right there and keep your hands where I can see them. My partner will come in after you."

"He can't. The door's locked. That's why I had to break the window."

"Who do you think you're kidding? How did you come in through a locked door? You got keys?"

"If I had keys I wouldn't have had to break the window. I was knocked out and tied up in here and the guy who did it took care to lock me in as well."

"What for?"

"Talking this way, we'll never know what for. If you'll just hold it long enough to let me tell you who I am and what the situation is, we can get moving on what we have to do here. Otherwise we're stuck. You're asking the impossible. If I had any way of getting out of here, I'd have been out long ago. You came around here because somebody phoned in a squeal. Someone said they were passing through the street and heard a man breaking a window and yelling like crazy for help and for the police. You came to investigate, didn't you?"

"So what?"

"So I've been yelling for you."

"You or some other guy? Like some guy you were leaning on?"

We were still getting nowhere. I skipped the answer he was anticipating and instead I threw at him my name and my DA's office connection.

"That," he said, "is a new one. Mostly they're the Mayor's best buddy and don't we want to keep our badge?"

I showed him my empty hands.

"Look," I said. "You have the light on me. You have me blinded with it. You can see me and I can't see anything but glare. You have your gun on me as well. What can you lose? Just give me the okay on going into my pocket for my ID."

"Nothing doing," he said. "You come up here. Push up against the bars."

I did as he told me. He grabbed himself a handful of my shirt and pulled hard. He might have been trying to pull me through the bars by main force. "Okay," he continued. "Now you grab the bars with your hands like you was a monkey and this here was your cage and you hold yourself right there tight against the bars."

I played along, savoring the thought that this was going to be a sorry cop as soon as he stopped playing games and let himself find out who I was.

"Like this, Officer?" I asked.

"That's right. Hands holding onto the bars where I can see them, and keep them there. Now you tell me which pocket."

I indicated the pocket. He reached in and brought out my billfold. I'd been thinking that flipping it open and taking a quick glance at my identification would be all he would need. But then he wasn't hurrying it. He took a long look at the ID and then he turned his light full on my face and took a long look at me. Perhaps he was just being careful, making certain of the match of picture to face before he was going to allow himself to relax, or perhaps he was not taking all that much convincing and he was just playing a game of being super-careful while he figured out the best way he could have for climbing down from the position he had taken.

Either way, I found my resentment evaporating. From where he stood it couldn't have been easy to believe that I was what I said I was or even that the ID I had on me was my own. If what he had in his hand was a stolen billfold complete with stolen papers, it wouldn't have been the first in his or any other cop's experience.

"I'm sorry, sir," he said as he handed my billfold out for me to retrieve. "How could I know?"

Obviously I was no longer required to keep my hands where he could see them. I took the billfold and dropped it back into my pocket.

"You couldn't," I told him. "You handled it the only possible way."

Things go better if you keep the Policemen's Benevolent Association benevolent.

The cops stayed with me. Using their squad-car radio, they relayed my messages into headquarters. The desk boys would get through to Henderson and keep us briefed on progress. While we waited, I filled the cops in on further details. I also had a new thought. If they passed me a flashlight through the bars, I could do a far more effective exploration of the building than I had been able to manage on what little street light filtered in through the windows.

"I can start a check on whether he left us anything," I suggested. "There just could be some evidence around to indicate what it was he was doing here."

"You're sure he's gone, sir? You're sure you'll be all right in there? With us here we can figure he won't come out to the window, but once you move away from us . . ."

The officer left it hanging. He wasn't ready to say right out that he doubted my ability to take care of myself, but the suggestion was obvious.

I reassured him. If I could find nothing else, there was a good possibility of my locating the fuse box and bringing the lights back on. They were nervous about it, but on my insistence they did pass me a flashlight. I went off and explored. The fuse box wasn't hard to find. It was at the back of the entrance hall, set in the wall under the stairs. Its covering door stood open and all the fuses were in the sockets. They hadn't been removed. They had only been loosened. It took only a couple of moments to screw them up tight and, when I returned to the light switches by the front door, I was able to flip the lights on.

The lighted hall showed me nothing but a few spots of blood dried on the stairs. I wasted no time over that. It was some of mine, just a little more of what I'd already felt matted in my hair.

I went on through the building, upstairs and down, hitting all the offices and switching the lights on everywhere. On the surface of things I could detect nothing amiss. Someone who was familiar with the place was going to have to look it over for evidence of what my assailant had been doing there. All I found was further evidence of what I already knew. The man was thorough. He overlooked nothing. Before he'd gone out of there and locked the door on me, he too had covered the whole building. Right through the place, in every one of the offices, there was not a phone anywhere that hadn't had its cords severed.

I did, however, locate one room I couldn't check. The door to that one was locked, as was a service door I found in the basement. That service door, of course, like the front door, would lead to the street. Of all the interior doors, however, there was only this one locked one. If such evidence as I was looking for was to be found, I thought, it would be behind that locked door.

Whatever was in there was going to have to keep. I went back to my broken window. The cops gave me the report from HQ.

They had found Henderson's home number and were working on it but were getting no answer. While they were telling me this, a further report came in. Getting nothing on Henderson, the boys on the department switchboard had tried the other partner, one Everett Crown.

On the Crown phone, they were reporting, they did get an answer, but it was nothing that would do us any good. Everett, the Crown half of Henderson & Crown, was not at home. His wife answered and said she couldn't tell the boys where her husband could be reached. All she could promise was that she would leave him a note and he would be in touch with headquarters as soon as he got home. She was going back to sleep. The call had wakened her and we could gather from the report that came to us that she hadn't liked being wakened.

That was hard cheese. I wasn't liking the way my night was going either. I had one more idea of something I could try before I would tell the cops to crash the door in. People do have duplicate keys. Lots of men keep duplicate sets in their desks. It was worth a try. I had no shortage of desks I could explore and I now had proper light to do it by.

Actually I didn't have many desks. Most of those I tried were locked, but then I came on one that wasn't locked and in it I hit pay dirt, a key ring with so many keys on it that it might well have done for unlocking every door for blocks around. I hurried back to the front door and had a try on that. It took a little doing before I had located the right keys, but they were there and it wasn't too long before I had the door swung open.

So then I had company. One of the cops stayed with the squad car, but the other joined me inside the building. He was all set to break down that one interior door that was locked, but I'd been too successful with the keys not to make another try with them. This door was easier. It had only the one lock, and that the standard job almost any key will work. I found one. It did work, but behind it we came up with nothing but the telephone switchboard. It took no more than a quick glance at the switchboard to explain the locked door. My man knew all he needed to know about ordinary phones. Cut the cord and you have them out of service. He hadn't known that much about switchboards. Hesitating over which cord to cut and fearful that he might not succeed in putting it out of commission, he had settled for locking the door on it.

On the switchboard phone I promptly got a dial tone. Posted above the board was a list of numbers the operator would want to keep always before her. It included home numbers for Ralph Henderson and Everett Crown. I tried the Henderson number and did no better than the boys down in headquarters. I got no answer.

I tried the Crown number. There the answer was so quick that it cut off the first ring at what must have been its very beginning. Only if someone was sitting with his hand on the instrument and every muscle tensed to snatch it up the moment it began ringing could you have a response that instantaneous.

"Hello!"

The voice was a woman's. It was shrill and strained. It was at once loud and choked. It vibrated with a barely controlled tremolo of jangled nerves.

"Everett Crown, please," I said.

The voice caught in what sounded like a muffled sob.

"Who's calling?" the woman asked.

Have you ever heard a quiet scream? It's a special sound. It has none of the noise of a scream and all of the intensity. Her question was just such a quiet scream.

"District Attorney's office," I said.

That evoked a full-voiced scream, nothing quiet about that one.

"You're the police or something like the police," she ranted, "so it's no good my telling you that if you don't stop bothering me, I'll call the police, but there must be something a person can do to stop being molested this way. Do I have to plead with you? I'm trying to sleep. I'm desperate for sleep. Hang up and don't call here again. Never again."

"Is this Mrs. Crown?"

I tried to get the words slipped in past her screen of hysteria.

"Yes. This is Mrs. Crown and someone's locked up in the office and you need the keys to get him out. I've had all that from the police and I've already told them I couldn't help them. Break down the door. Knock down the whole damn building for all I care, but stop bothering me. Just let me sleep. Can't you understand that?"

"I'm sorry, Mrs. Crown," I began.

She didn't wait for me to finish.

"You're sorry," she stormed, breaking in on me. "You're not too sorry to go on and on at me. I can't help you. I told the police I can't help you. I'm hanging up and, for God's sake, don't ring this phone again. Leave me alone. Please, please, leave me alone."

"Give me some other number I can call," I said, trying to make another beginning.

I wanted to suggest that if she could direct me to someone who would know the office, an office manager or a chief clerk—someone like that—I could stop bothering her. She didn't wait for it. She hung up on me. By the sound of it, she banged the instrument down into its cradle, taking out on it what she evidently wanted to do to me.

I hung up as well and for a moment or two I just sat, staring at the switchboard and thinking about the way voices sound over the telephone. Hers could have been the hysterical voice of a tortured insomniac whose fragile hold on sleep had been twice shattered by the telephone and who was now grappling with a fear that sleep would never come to her again. It was possible but it seemed to me that it was no more possible than the line Ralph Henderson tried to sell me when he phoned to call off the appointment he had only slightly earlier been so passionately urging on me.

All too similarly it now seemed to me that his partner's wife had not been wakened by my call. I wasn't even ready to believe that she had been wakened by the earlier call she'd had from the police. To me she sounded like a woman who had not and would not sleep that night. The instant reaction with which she snatched up the phone even before it had fairly begun ringing seemed in itself significant. This was a woman who in some agony of anxiety was waiting at the phone in expectation of a vital call. If it wasn't that, it would have to be a timing accident by which I caught her just as she was picking up the phone to put through some call she considered most urgent.

The lady knew what had been going on in the Henderson & Crown offices that night or at least she was possessed of background knowledge which made it easy for her to make an educated guess. All too much like her husband's partner, Ralph Henderson, the lady most desperately wanted the police and the DA's office kept out of it. Learning that we were this much into it hadn't pleased her, but now she was merely doing what she could. She was giving us nothing. It was even possible that she wanted us off her phone so that she might use it to spread a warning that we were not as much out of Henderson & Crown affairs as had been hoped.

I studied the list of names and phone numbers posted above the switchboard. There were many other names and numbers listed along with Ralph Henderson's and Everett Crown's but nothing to indicate who these other people might be. I could expect there would be included home numbers for top employees such as an office manager or the top private secretary, but for the moment I was at a loss for any way to distinguish such from outsiders with whom the firm did some good part of its business.

One name on the list, however, did jump out at me. On the list it appeared as "Mr. Dryden," and I wondered why that particular one should be riveting my attention. The long-dead poet had never had a telephone number and I couldn't recall ever having known of any other Dryden. I tried to pass it by in the hope of finding something on the list that might look more promising, but it seemed to be pushing itself at me.

I had seen that name somewhere. It wasn't fresh in my mind. I wasn't having any luck with placing it, but it was fresh just at the outer edge of my consciousness. Then I was struck with an idea about it. Even if my idea didn't work out for Dryden, it might be useful for some other name on the switchboard list. I went back through the offices I had already explored.

I hadn't previously taken any particular notice of it, but now I did see that on each of the more imposing desks there was a brass name plate to identify the occupant. I located R. Henderson and E. Crown. Just down the hall from Ralph Henderson's office I came on Dryden. It was A. Dryden.

Returning to the switchboard, I dialed the Dryden number. The answer came quickly. It wasn't the instantaneous pickup I'd had from Mrs. Crown, but it was quick. The man who answered didn't say hello and he didn't wait for his caller to identify himself. He behaved as though it could have been only one person calling him.

"Baby," he said as he picked up the phone. "And it's about time. I was beginning to wonder how I could manage to give up loving you."

"Mr. Dryden," I interrupted, trying to save the man the embarrassment of going any further with that.

He broke in on my interruption.

"I don't have to worry about how to give up loving you, mister," he said. "Whoever you are, I hate you."

5

I SQUEEZED INTO THAT with my identification; but, aside from putting a halt to the chitchat, it didn't do me much good. I explained that I was trying to reach someone who would know how to put me in touch with Ralph Henderson or Everett Crown and who could do something about it immediately.

He did sober down and tell me he was just my man. He was Ralph Henderson's secretary.

"Nine in the morning," he said. "Mr. Henderson is always at his desk right on the dot. I'll tell him you'd like him to call you first thing."

"Morning," I said, "will almost certainly be too late. I must reach him right now. Failing Henderson, Crown might do, but one or the other just as quickly as you can locate him."

"Where can I get back to you?" he asked. "I don't like to this time of night, but I'll try them at home. Are you at your office?"

"No," I said. "I'm at yours and I've been trying both of them on their home numbers. On Henderson we've been getting no answer. For Crown we've been getting the Mrs. and she's been no help at all. She just flies into a temper over our waking her. Crown isn't home and all she says she can do is leave him a message he'll find when he comes in. Meanwhile she's going back to sleep."

He listened to all that without offering any interruptions and, when I paused in the hope that he might be coming up with something, the pause just strung itself out. He was saying nothing.

I tried pushing a little. "Even if you don't have any ideas on where Ralph and his partner may be right now," I said, "you might do better with getting over to Mrs. Crown some idea of the great urgency."

I paused again, waiting for him to come up with something, but there was again only more of that silence. If it weren't that I could hear his breathing at the other end of the line, I might have thought we'd been cut off.

"You still there?" I asked, only to drag some sort of response out of the man.

"Perhaps," he said, "if you could give me some idea of the nature of your business with Henderson and Crown."

"District Attorney's office business," I snapped.

"And you're in our offices?"

"At your switchboard."

"With a warrant?"

"What would I need a warrant for?"

"You tell me. I'd have to ask a lawyer."

"I'm a friend of Ralph Henderson's. Let's stop horsing around."

"Will you be there for a while?"

"On the speed at which you move, Mr. Dryden," I told him, "I could be here forever."

The crack didn't seem to bother him at all.

"You hang on," he said. "I'll work my other phone and try to get through to someone. I'm sure I can get you something. Don't hang up."

I hung on, wondering a little about his other phone. One or more extensions on a line people do have and not so uncommonly that it should astonish anyone; but more than one line in a man's home is not so usual that, for a man who worked as a private secretary, it didn't seem too big-time.

From time to time Dryden came back to me. It was always brief. He was checking on whether I was still there. He was furnishing me progress reports. He too had tried to raise Ralph Henderson on his home phone and he too had been unsuccessful. No answer.

"I guess he hasn't gone home tonight," he offered. "You hang on. There are other numbers I can try."

I hung on, but when I next heard, it was from the cop who had stayed with the squad car. He came inside to fill me in. The man Dryden hadn't been trying to reach Ralph Henderson anywhere. He had just been stringing me along to hold me on the phone while over his other line he had reached the police to have them trace my call.

"They been telling the clown we ain't no practical joke and we ain't no mugs luring him down here so we can make him open up the safe for us," the cop explained. "That's what he's been figuring. Now he knows, maybe he'll get on the ball."

Dryden came back on. "I'm not having any luck," he said.

There was no point in playing games with the man. I told him what I'd heard from the police. I told him it was okay. I could understand him wanting to check me out before he would let me suck him out onto any limbs, but now he knew and he could start leveling with me.

"So let's have it, Dryden," I said. "Have you made any calls? Have you tried to reach anybody? Where do we stand?"

I liked the way he responded to that, no stammering or stuttering, not even the first word of apology or explanation. This man was a competent operator and he had all the cool self-assurance a man develops out of a knowledge of his own competence. His procedure with me had been eminently correct and he could hope that I would be man enough to recognize as much and take no offense. If I wasn't man enough, that was just too bad. I could go to hell.

"I can't get anything on Mr. Henderson's number," he said. "That's where I made my first try and when I found I couldn't talk to him about you, I took it on my own responsibility to check you out. Since then I've tried the only other number I know. It's Mr. Henderson's club and that's no good. He isn't there and they haven't seen him at all tonight."

"No other numbers?" I asked. "Even a number where you wouldn't ordinarily disturb him?"

"If you're telling me this isn't ordinarily, I already know that, sir. I have no other numbers for him."

"What about Crown?"

"I wake Mrs. Crown this time?"

"On the chance that she'll talk to you even though she won't to us."

"Okay," he sighed. "I'll try her and I'll call you back."

"Try her on your other phone. I'll hold on."

"Right," he said. "Mr. Henderson or Mr. Crown, either one, if she can give us any lead on where we can reach one or the other of them real quick."

"And if she can't help that way, maybe she'll tell you what she has on her mind. When she talks to us, she says she hasn't a thing bugging her but getting back to sleep, and it isn't that. She's a lady who's sitting up late and holding her breath."

"Do you know the lady?" Dryden asked.

"Only the one moment of talk on the phone, and that was all 'go away and stop bothering me.' "

"On what I know of her, getting back to sleep is just the kind of thing that would worry her," Dryden said. "She'd hate anything to interfere with her rest."

"If it runs you into trouble," I promised him, "I'll cover for you. What can you do, after all? I'm pressuring you."

"Oh, that's okay," he said, speaking out of what sounded like an impregnable cool. "I work for Mr. Henderson. I'm answerable only to Mr. Henderson. He'll back me all the way. It's just that I hate it when women scream at me, and from what you say . . ."

"Hate it or not," I said, "I am pressuring you."

"Yeah," he said. "I been noticing. Hang on. Here we go."

And this time it was different. He evidently had one of his phones on a jack or on a long cord. Previously, during all the time I'd been hanging on and he had been working his other phone, I'd heard not a single sound, neither the buzzes and clicks of his dialing nor even the faintest and most distant murmur of what he'd been saying. Now he obviously had the two telephone instruments side by side. I could listen to his dialing. I heard him spin the thing for eight digits. It was one followed by a pause and then in rapid grouping the customary seven. He was hooked to an apartment house or hotel switchboard then. That first digit took him to an outside line and brought him his dial tone. He had the two instruments cheek by jowl. I could even hear the dial tone when he brought it in. I also heard Mrs. Crown's receiver come off the hook. Dryden hated it when women screamed at him. I could guess that he had taken the precaution of holding his receiver just that small distance away from his ear, just enough to offer him some hope of coming away from the phone with a still usable eardrum.

I could hear the first ring and how it was again aborted before it was fairly begun. I could hear her hello and, if when I'd had her on the phone she had sounded all but out of control, she had in the interval made no noticeable recovery. Again this was a woman who stood only a moment away from going violently mad.

Dryden hurried into the breach. "Al Dryden here, Mrs. Crown," he said.

There was a moment of dead silence. It had to be that the lady was gathering herself together for something. She could have been mustering all her strength to blast him with a fury that would make what she had turned on me seem like nothing at all. I suppose I had accepted that as so much the likeliest possibility that I'd hardly bothered to think of anything else. After that moment of silence, however, she did speak and it was something else. She had been bracing herself to ask a question which, from the sound of her, she had hardly dared ask. Whether it was because she was so fearful of what the answer might be or so hopeful I had no way of judging.

"You've heard from Ralph?" she asked, and there could be no doubt about it. Behind that question she was throwing everything she had into pleading with Dryden to tell her that he had. "He's given you a message for me, Allen. Tell me, please, tell me. Don't keep me waiting."

Since at the beginning of that her voice had already been up there at the level of a scream, it might now have been without any place to go. It was, nevertheless, on its way. It was soaring well up into the level of superscream.

"No, Mrs. Crown," Dryden told her. "I'm sorry, Mrs. Crown, I haven't heard from Mr. Henderson at all. Not from Mr. Henderson and not from Mr. Crown. I'm trying to locate them or at least one of them. It's necessary for me to reach them as quickly as possible. You see, Mrs. Crown, something most peculiar has been going on down at the office tonight and they should know about it."

She did permit him to go that far with it before she let him have it, but then the blast came. Hearing it even as I was, filtered through two telephone connections, I had no trouble recognizing it for something NASA would have liked to take down to Cape Kennedy. Set up on a pad down there, it could have carried the boys what my great-grandmother used to call a far piece.

"I know about the office," she screamed, "and you don't have to keep my phone tied up babbling about it. Get off the line and stay off. Forget about the office. Go to sleep. Go find yourself a girl if you can't sleep, but for God's sake stay away from the office, stay away from me, and stay off my phone. If you can think of any way to get the police to forget about us, do it. Get them away from the office. I don't care how you do it, Allen, but do what you can, please, and now get off my phone and stay off."

"But, Mrs. Crown," Dryden said, attempting to give it another try.

"But nothing," the lady screamed. "I don't know where you can reach them. I don't know where you can reach anybody, and if I did know, I wouldn't tell you. Wild horses wouldn't drag it out of me. The police wouldn't. Even if it meant the rest of my life in jail. So can't you see it's no good not leaving me alone? I know nothing and if I get to know anything, I won't tell you or them or anyone. So it's futile. You're accomplishing nothing and you're torturing me. So, please, Allen, please, no more. Hang up. Leave me alone."

I heard her hang up on him. I heard the dial tone come back on. I could visualize him with the telephone still in his hand. He would be staring at it, so busy with his thoughts that he was forgetting to return it to its cradle. Then he did remember. I heard the click of the thing dropping into place and the cessation of the dial tone. I expected he would come right back on to me, but he didn't. Obviously he was giving himself a couple of moments for further thinking. It wasn't what I wanted of him. I shouted into the phone, hoping I could get into my voice something of that same degree of penetration as Mrs. Crown had put into her screaming. Maybe I had some measure of success and maybe Allen

Dryden came back to me of his own accord. I had no way of knowing.

"No luck," he said. "I've been talking to Mrs. Crown and she hasn't the first clue to where we might try to reach either of them. She's even worse off for leads then I was. At least I knew I could try Mr. Henderson's club. She didn't know even that much. Of course, as it happens, it did me no good, but it was the one lead I did have and she has none."

When she had accused him of babbling she had been something less than fair, but now the charge was coming to look like a self-fulfilling prophecy. Allen Dryden was babbling.

I chopped him right down out of that. "She doesn't know," I said, "and if she did, neither your wild horses nor my police could ever drag it out of her. Also now you are to persuade us to leave the Henderson and Crown offices and to forget we'd ever been there."

"You heard all of that," he murmured. "I suppose I should have called her the way I made the other calls, from the other room."

"If you made a mistake," I told him, "it was one of those mistakes that turns out all too well. This one takes you off the hook. You don't have to worry over whether or not company loyalty requires that you tell me what she said or that you keep the word from me. I overheard. It's out of your hands."

"Look," he said, breaking in on me. "Do you have any idea at all what's going on? Mrs. Crown knows and she says I'm to keep out of it, but I don't think that's enough. I'd have to hear that from Mr. Henderson himself. Not even Mr. Crown could quite do it so far as I am concerned, much less the lady."

"You'd better get over here," I told him. "There must be something out of line and you'll spot it. We're unfamiliar with the office and we're just not seeing it."

It was couched as a suggestion but I'd expected it to be taken as an order. It wasn't. He had questions. He gave evidence of wanting to discuss.

"Then you're spotting nothing obvious?" he murmured. "No signs of tampering with the safe? Of trying to break into it or anything like that? Desk drawers forced open? Anything of that sort?"

"How long will it take you to get your clothes on and come over here?" I asked.

"I live near," he said. "I've been dressing all the time I've been on the phone. Everything's on, so I'll be there in two minutes. If I can get lucky with a cab it will be less than that."

He did get lucky. He came in a cab and his time was almost as good as he'd promised. At first sight of him, however, I thought I might have been the victim of some sort of trick. A switch had been pulled on me. The weirdo who came hurtling out of the cab just couldn't possibly have been Allen Dryden, secretary to Ralph Henderson. Nobody who looked like that could ever be employed by any firm that built its image on the eminently correct decor of the Henderson & Crown offices.

Henderson was every inch the staid, conservative, solid businessman. If a man like Henderson had a male secretary, it could only be that even the most businesslike of businesswomen would have seemed too fluttery and flighty to him and that he could be content with nothing less than the full rigidity of a Harvard Business School type.

So what is this Dryden? He's the complete kook. He's way out. It wasn't that I hadn't seen his like before. I was even accustomed to them. They're all over town and they're very much in business. They run off-Broadway theaters. They operate art cinemas. They decorate show windows. They create hair styles. They run boutiques and little restaurants. Eat at a place called The Nonchalant Noodle and they'll be waiting on table, but they don't work as secretaries in offices where the carefully cultivated look is that of a nineteenth-century British countinghouse. The atmosphere of the offices was not Carnaby Street. It was Threadneedle.

This young man who was introducing himself as Allen Dryden, secretary to Ralph Henderson, had hair that hung down to the level of the hinges of his jaws, bangs that caressed his eyebrows, and sideburns that were only a small fraction of an inch shorter than the hair that tended to fall so far forward on his face that it threatened to conceal them.

At the other end of him it was the inevitable sandals and no socks and down there I noticed the only thing about him that could have been called atypical. As seen through the interstices of his sandals his feet were clean. For feet even partially bared to city streets that's phenomenal any time. The areas between sandals and hair were completely tie-dyed, a T-shirt that gave the effect of white patterning on black and trousers that appeared to be black-patterned on white. You could give Rorschach tests with those jeans. If either shirt or britches had been any tighter, they would have been subcutaneous. As it was, you could have sworn he didn't have a thing on under either, not even skin.

He just wasn't to be believed, at least not in the secretary-to-Henderson context. Nevertheless he had to be believed. As soon as he spoke, and that was the moment he leaped from the cab, the voice and the accent were unmistakable. This was the man I'd had on the phone. This was also a man divided. On one side you had the clothes, the hair and the sandals. In contradistinction you had his manner, his deportment, his incisiveness, his efficiency and his clean feet. Everything he did and everything in the way he did it indicated the perfect secretary, the lad who knew his way around the world of business and who was an effective operator in that world, even at its power-wielding levels. He was all efficiency, aplomb and self-confidence. Watching him as he walked in and took hold, I could almost believe that I had lost track of how business is done these days and that somehow while I wasn't looking IBM's starched white collars had come to this. The boy was so much the proper secretary that if he was wearing it, it had to be proper secretary's garb.

He was methodical, taking each item as he came to it. He began with the front door, examining both door and frame, checking the locks, looking for gouged wood or scratched paint.

"Obviously the door wasn't forced," he said. "Since I was the last to leave yesterday and I did the locking up, it has to mean that whoever was in here had keys."

"You locked all the locks?" I said.

"Most carefully," he said.

"Who lets the cleaning women in?"

"Nobody. They have their own keys. They just come in."

"So what you did about locking up," I said, "isn't material. We'll have to know whether the cleaning women were careful to lock up after themselves tonight."

He shook his head. "They couldn't be more responsible," he told me. "They've been with us for years and they're utterly reliable, but tonight it's beside the point. I worked late. They were finished and gone before I knocked off. So I was the last to leave. I locked up."

"What time was that?"

"Seven to seven-fifteen."

"Would you know if someone was coming back to put in some extra time during the evening?"

"I would expect to know it."

"Mr. Henderson?"

"That I would definitely know. Anytime he's coming in he asks me to come in, too."

"But not tonight?"

"Not tonight."

6

As THE YOUNG FELLOW went through the place, it seemed to me that I'd never known anyone who gave a stronger impression of being sharp-eyed and alert. As he moved from office to office, it was obvious that he had a complete familiarity with every inch of this ground he was covering. If there would be even the smallest item out of line he was going to notice it.

I kept hoping there would be something. Steadily my expectations rose and quite as steadily they were dashed. In addition to the sharp alertness which obviously could never miss a thing, Dryden displayed such a talent for detection and so striking a gift for bringing together even meager evidence to produce a logical deduction as I would never have expected from him. It was this part of his performance that brought me my rising expectations. I had every good reason for believing that if and when he came on the revealing item he would milk out of it for me its every possible revelation. What was dashing me was that our inspection tour was bringing us nothing more than a dead zero. Dryden was coming up with nothing I hadn't already discovered on my own.

There were a few items I had to explain to him, but that was only because they were no longer the way my assailant had left them. I had returned the fuses to their sockets, restoring the electric power and, until I explained that detail to Dryden, he was disquieted by the electric clocks. He noticed that they were all running behind time and by almost identical intervals. I bring this up only as an example of how observant he was and how surefooted in his processes of reasoning from the evidence.

I was about to tell him that they were all off by the same interval but he went straight ahead and demonstrated to me that they weren't. The differences were so small that I would have expected anyone who even noticed them to dismiss them as negligible, but Dryden had taken note of them and from the differences he had drawn his conclusions.

"Taking the extremes," he said, "we have two clocks that show times more than two minutes apart with the others varying within those limits. That means power was out on all lines in the building, but the cutoff point couldn't have been at the level of the trunk line that feeds in from the street. It had to be at our fuse box. It was killed there line by line and restored there line by line. That would give us this sort of variation unless the fuses were pulled and put back by someone working in the same order and at the same speed."

Impressed with the man, I told him how precisely right he was. Satisfied then in the area of the clocks, he switched his concern to the telephones. Since he could make no sense of them, they troubled him.

"Every phone in the place put out of commission," he grumbled, "and the switchboard left working."

I filled him in on that piece of the puzzle, telling him that the only locked room in the place had been the one that housed the switchboard.

"Yes," he said. "And that tells us something more. We can eliminate all people like switchboard operators who know the way the thing works. We're narrowed down to people like me."

"The switchboard room?" I asked. "Is it customarily left unlocked?"

"With the one obvious exception of doors to johns," Dryden said, "I don't know of any time when any interior door in this whole place was ever locked. I'm surprised at anyone around here even remembering there was a key."

"Anyone around here," I said, echoing his words. "You keep assuming an insider." I was assuming as much myself but I wanted to hear his thinking on it. It could reflect some bit of evidence I didn't have. He ran through his reasoning for me.

"As I understand it," he said, "given the know-how and the equipment, a man can pick any lock made and get it open. Maybe you know. The locks on the street door have to be closed with keys. They aren't spring locks. I assume they could be opened with a pick lock. Does it work both ways? Could a pick lock have been used to lock them up again?"

"I heard the door shut," I told him, "and I heard the locks ram home. That was done with keys. It was too quick for anything else, even if anything else should prove possible."

He shrugged. "So there you are," he said. "An insider. Nobody else has keys."

"And among the insiders?" I asked. "Everybody who works here has them?"

He shook his head and began ticking off on his fingers the holders of keys. The two partners, Ralph Henderson and Everett Crown, two cleaning women for nights he didn't work late and they had to lock up after themselves, the janitor and a porter because one or the other of them was always first to arrive in the morning.

"Emily and me," he finished. "That's the lot."

"Who's Emily?"

"Emily Johnson. She's Mr. Crown's secretary."

"And all of you have complete sets, even to the key to the switchboard room?" I asked.

"No," he began, "not that one. I didn't know that anyone . . ." Even while he was saying the words, some doubt of what he was saying took them and rammed them back into his throat. His voice faded away. When it came back to him, it was asking a question. "You checked desk drawers and found a spare set of keys," he said. "With those keys you got the front door open and you unlocked the door in here and got at the switchboard. Where did you find those keys?"

"The only place I could have found them," I said.

"Right. In my desk, because there isn't another desk around here that isn't kept locked. That's just what I've been thinking and I could swear that there was nothing on that key ring but office keys—front door, service door, and doors to Mr. Henderson's office and mine."

He seemed to be listing more keys than I'd found on that spare set I'd taken from his desk drawer and that without the one I knew it included, the one I had used to unlock the switchboard room. I showed him the keys. He identified them one by one, matching them up to their various locks and finishing with the one in question.

"This one," he said. "It opens my door and Mr. Henderson's. And I'm a dope. I knew it also opens Mr. Crown's door and

Emily's except that it's never used because none of our doors is ever locked. But that's it. It opens all the interior doors, the switchboard room as well."

"And this spare set is always in the same drawer in your desk and the drawer is always left unlocked?"

He explained that it was just because of this spare set of keys that he always left his desk unlocked. There would have been little point in having an extra set available for emergencies if they weren't available at all times.

All the time we were kicking around these questions about the keys we were giving it only part of our attention. Dryden, at the same time, was covering all the offices, checking out all of what he evidently took to be the critical locations, such as desks an invader might have been interested in rifling, files he might have had reason to invade, the office safe.

Keys the man carried on him were obviously a much more extensive set than those left in his desk for emergencies. With keys from his pocket he unlocked filing cabinets and did quick inspections of their contents, he unlocked the desks of the two partners and rapidly scanned what they contained, and he even unlocked that remaining executive-suite desk, the one that belonged to Everett Crown's secretary. He said he could see no indication of anything having been touched in any of the files or any of the desks.

"Are all of you always in and out of each other's things this way?" I asked. "Do you all carry keys to everything? No privacy for anybody?"

"Everybody's in and out of my desk all the time," he explained. "If I have anything I don't want everybody pawing over, I lock it away in one of the files or I take it home with me. Otherwise Emily and Mr. Crown have keys to each other's desks. I think Mr. Henderson does have a key to mine, but since mine is never locked, it just hasn't come up, so I'm not quite certain of that."

"And for real privacy everyone takes stuff home?" I asked.

Dryden grinned. "Can do," he said, "but I'd be the last to know. Since I'm everybody's buddy around here, the man everyone trusts, I've always assumed that nobody would be interested in hiding anything away from me. Nobody's ever made any moves toward setting up a place where stuff might be locked away from me. So that's the way it would have to be. If anybody around here isn't trusting me, I guess they would be keeping stuff at home."

These answers of his were interesting enough, but they weren't diverting me from keeping a sharp watch on what he was doing. When he looked into the desks and when he checked the files, he opened things up and really looked, but he didn't open everything up. In the files that would have taken months, and the impression he gave me was that he knew the stuff so well that he could pinpoint the areas that might hold a clue and bypass all the rest of the material while he concentrated on what had the potential of proving relevant. When he came to the office safe, however, he merely glanced at it and turned away.

"And that hasn't been touched either," he said. "I'm licked. I can't figure what it could have been you interrupted."

"How do you know the safe hasn't been touched?" I asked. "You haven't opened it. You've hardly looked at it."

"I know. I'd rather not say how I know."

"You don't want to open it?"

"If you insist," he muttered. "It's a waste of time since nobody's touched it, but that's all right. Here goes."

It may have been deliberate—the act of a careful man whose view of his responsibility for company property was so serious that he was not taking any chances on even the DA's office picking up the safe combination—or it could have been automatic, just the cautious man's longtime habit into which he fell without even being aware that he was doing it. In any event he placed himself so that all view of the safe was screened away from me all the time he was twirling the combination dial. It wasn't until he had swung the door open that he stepped aside to let me see.

What he revealed was a picture of the most orderly precision.

"I'm always neating it up after the others," he said. "You can see for yourself there isn't even one paper that needs neating up in here now. Nobody's been at it."

This expressed conviction, however, didn't stand in the way of his doing some checking. Here, too, as in the files, he had his selected areas he seemed to feel warranted inspection. He brought out one ledger, flipped it open and glanced at a couple of its pages. Returning that to the safe, he took out a cash box. Opening it, he counted the money it contained, a little over three thousand dollars. Returning the money to the box and the box to the safe, he declared triumphantly that it was all just as he'd said it would be. The safe hadn't been touched.

"You said you always neat up after the others," I reminded him. "Who are these others?"

His answer was the expected one. Four people knew and used the combination, the two partners and their respective secretaries.

"Emily Johnson," I said. "Is she likely to know anything you don't know?"

For a moment he looked as though the question had offended him. Obviously he thought of himself as a member of the inner circle at Henderson & Crown. He didn't care for the suggestion that another secretary, and a female one at that, might be more inner than himself. He forced himself to consider it.

"On company business," he said, "the answer would be no. I have Mr. Henderson's complete confidence. On any personal concern of Mr. Henderson's most emphatically not. In that area I know more even than Mr. Crown. Mr. Henderson has no family. I am closer to him than anyone else. That leaves something personal over at the Crowns. I wouldn't know much about that. I'd guess that Emily wouldn't either, but then again I'm not enough in either Mr. or Mrs. Crown's confidence to know how they feel about Emily. She always puts on a big act of being their best buddy, of course, but what else can she do? She's not about to let me know that she isn't as close to her boss as I am to Mr. Henderson."

He was shutting the safe. I left him to it. He was coming up with nothing. The police had been staying with the Henderson home phone number and were still getting no answer. I looked at my watch. It was shortly after one and I was surprised that it wasn't later. It hardly seemed possible that it had been only an hour since I'd freed myself and first looked at my watch. I felt as though I had been giving far more than an hour to this fever of futile activity. It occurred to me that Emily Johnson might be as avid for sleep as her boss's wife professed herself to be, but I wasn't going to let that worry me. For all of Dryden's self-importance he appeared to know nothing. Miss Johnson might prove more helpful. I could hardly imagine her being less helpful. Her number was, of course, one of those posted at the switchboard. I gave it a try. It rang for a considerable time before I had an answer. Then a sleepy voice came on. It was a woman's voice, but it wasn't Emily. It was her mother. Emily wasn't home. She was away for the night. No, Mama couldn't tell me where I could reach Emily, but when I explained that it was an office emergency, she said that if I gave her my number, she would have Emily call me back. It would be only a few moments.

I settled for that and waited for the return call. It was no more than the promised matter of moments. The phone rang just as Dryden came away from the safe and joined me.

I briefed him rapidly before I picked up the phone. He picked up another earset and plugged it in so he could listen with me.

It was Emily Johnson calling back and she sounded nothing like a secretary. If it hadn't been for Dryden identifying Emily's voice,

I would have wondered whether Mama Johnson wasn't foisting some ringer on me. Emily sounded almost as hysterical as her boss's wife. She was with Mrs. Crown. Mrs. Crown wasn't feeling well and Mr. Crown had been forced to go out. They had called Emily early in the evening and asked her to come over and spend the night with Mrs. Crown. Emily was doing just that. She was calling from the Crowns. She couldn't leave Mrs. Crown. She couldn't help me in any way. She recommended that we go away and sleep on the thing till we could take it up with Mr. Henderson and Mr. Crown in the morning. Meanwhile in the name of simple humanity would we stop ringing the Crown number? The poor woman was feeling very badly and we weren't helping at all by breaking up her sleep. Emily said all that and hung up. It was the package as before. Go away. Forget it. Get off Mrs. Crown's phone and if you have any human feelings at all, stay off.

So again I was left with no one but Allen Dryden. Since he had boasted that he more than anyone else had an intimate knowledge of Ralph Henderson's affairs, I tried him on anything he might have known about Henderson's plans for the evening. He insisted that he knew nothing. He also insisted that if there had been any plans, particularly any affair that had to do with the office, he would have known.

I knew that there had been something even if only something that was set up and later canceled. The young man was either overestimating the degree to which he was in his boss's confidence or else he was lying. I made a try at frightening something out of him.

"Henderson did have something on tonight," I said. "He insisted that it wasn't dangerous. He said he knew his man and he had no fear of the man going violent. Considering what happened to me when I came in here tonight, we know he was wrong on that point. I've been thinking that the whole reason for tying me up, killing the lights, killing the phones, and locking me in might have been to hold me out of action long enough for this man to get at Henderson. It could be too late even now, but the way the man fixed things it doesn't seem as though he wanted just a little time. It's more as though he wanted the whole night and if we don't find Henderson, it may well be that we're giving this man exactly what he wanted."

Dryden sighed. "And not a thing we can do," he said. "Certainly there's nothing here. I'm sorry I've been no help. Would you like me to lock up or are you going to hang on here?"

He wasn't saying it in so many words, but he was letting me know that he felt he had done everything in his power and he was now ready to cut out. More than that, he seemed suddenly eager to cut out.

"Nothing more for me here," I said. "The police will hang on. I can't imagine my man will be coming back, but just in case."

"Uh-huh," he muttered. "So if there's nothing more I can do for you, sir . . ."

"You have some place to go, Mr. Dryden?"

"I have an apartment. I have a bed. Your call pulled me out of it."

"And that's all?"

He didn't look sleepy. He didn't even look tired. My question made him look sheepish.

"When you called me," he said. "That routine I went into before you got to say anything. You don't think I go into that automatically every time my phone rings?"

"Nothing to be embarrassed about," I told him. "You'd been expecting a call. It never entered your mind that it wouldn't be that call. It could happen to anyone."

He grinned at me. "I had been expecting a visitor," he said. "I left her a note and came over here. I'm hoping she's been waiting for me, but I can't hope she'll wait indefinitely. They'll keep you waiting. They take it to be a privilege of their sex, but you keep them waiting and they take umbrage. Haven't you ever noticed that? Even if she was nothing special, I just don't do so well for choan that I can afford to let any of it get away, and she is special. So if it's all right with you."

A couple of times during that speech he shot nervous glances at his watch. They were ostentatiously the sort of glances Romeo might have taken at his hourglass if someone had tried to delay him on his way to the Capulet tomb. I thought I knew all the words, but choan was a new one to me. Since, however, its meaning seemed sufficiently clear from the context and since in any case it was not material to my concerns of the moment, I didn't ask him for any translations. Convinced that I had exhausted Dryden's usefulness and not being the man to place any impediments in the course of true love, I turned him loose. He was out of those offices like a greyhound unleashed.

7

I HAD TO TAKE a few minutes for setting things up in the Henderson & Crown offices before I could pull out of there. There was still too much in the situation that had about it the feeling of unfinished business. I couldn't lock the place up and just walk away from it. I wanted a police watch on the premises for the remainder of the night. So far as was possible I wanted it to be an inconspicuous watch. If my man was coming back, he wasn't to see anything that could warn him off. I had no way of knowing whether or not he would be coming back; but, if he did, I wanted him to walk into the arms of the police.

I hung on long enough to see a couple of detectives from the local precinct installed on the premises. They locked themselves in and killed all lights that might be seen from outside the building. There was nothing that could be done about my smashed window, but I hoped that, with no lights behind it, it might pass unnoticed. I watched the squad car pull away and then I took off.

There was only the one place I could go and I went there with divided feelings. Such part of me as was the investigator was hungry for answers. That other part of me, the human being, was hoping I'd find none. I was headed for the place where Ralph Henderson had his bachelor's quarters, the apartment where we had been keeping the phone ringing for what had now grown to a long time and where in all that time nobody had picked up a receiver.

I could imagine only two possibilities. One was that Ralph Henderson hadn't gone home that night. In that event I couldn't see how going around there was going to bring me any of those answers I wanted; but, as I was seeing it, the alternative to disappointment could only be tragedy. There was the second possibility: Ralph Henderson had gone home that night. I would find him in his apartment. His phone would be ringing unheeded, not because he wasn't there but because whatever of him was there would be in no condition for answering telephones.

Like his secretary, Henderson lived nearby. These were people who enjoyed the privilege of walking to work. The distance between office and home was so short that I covered it before I had even finished exploring all the possibilities I could develop out of my wishful thinking, much less make any sort of a beginning on all the rational objections that might have dented my hopes.

It was a Murray Hill apartment, a top-luxury deal in a top-luxury neighborhood. Buildings of this sort are heavily staffed. They have doormen and elevator operators and porters. In those early hours from one in the morning till about seven, however, the staff pares down to a single man. The building is locked up and he is there for the benefit of the resident who comes in late from a night on the town or who for some extraordinary reason takes off from the building on an unnaturally early start. He is also there in case of emergencies. For those deep-in-the-night hours he is the man of all work.

When I came to the building, its nightman was at his station. He appeared to be deep in a book, but before I could as much as touch the front door, he had seen me. Dropping his book, he sprang to the door, but only to inspect me through the glass. He made no move to open up for me. The manner in which he inspected me, surveying my person slowly and attentively from head to foot and then making the return journey to my head with an equally sharp scrutiny, it became evident that he wasn't liking what he saw. There was an intercom deal between lobby and vestibule and over that he asked me what I wanted.

"Mr. Henderson," I said. "Ralph Henderson."

"You expected?"

For handling that I identified myself, and with every word I threw at him the man took on a more noncommittally wooden look. He wasn't ready to say he didn't believe a word of what I was telling him, but he obviously wanted to keep that locked door between us for as long as it might take for me to give up on it and go away. Out there in the vestibule I had on both sides of me mirrored walls. Out of the corner of my eye I caught just enough of my reflection to give me a hint of what was troubling this night porter.

I hadn't forgotten any part of what I'd been through that night, but I'd been too much preoccupied with more pressing aspects of the situation to have given any thought to what the struggle and the subsequent captivity had done to my appearance.

I turned to take a quick look. My face could have been worse, but here and there it was noticeably knobby with swellings and here and there it had developed some lurid touches of color. My clothes were rumpled and showed some rips. Also some blood had shaken out of my hair to run down on my collar. It was no great quantity of blood, but for leaving ugly stains to dry on your clothes a few drops of the stuff will go a long way. I had to recognize it. I looked like no sort of arm of the law. I looked like a drunk who had taken a bad fall off the curb and had been rolling around in the gutter.

I didn't try to explain it. I brought out my ID and held it against the glass for him to read. It worked. He unlocked the door and admitted me to the lobby. Before dealing further with me, however, he stopped to lock the door. He was a careful man and serious about the responsibilities of his job.

"Is Mr. Henderson in his apartment?" I asked.

"No, but there is somebody up there if you want to go up."

I wanted more than ever to go up, but I also wanted to know what I'd be walking into.

"Who?" I asked.

"Mr. Dryden, Mr. Henderson's secretary. He comes around a lot. He has a key. I just took him up. I only just came down from taking him up."

"I know Mr. Dryden," I said. "I'll go up."

So now I had a small time lag to think about. When I had last seen Dryden, he had been moving at top speed, presumably stopping for nothing. Now the porter was telling me the man had come to the apartment only just before me. I could add up my delays. Some time had gone to setting up the police watch in the Henderson & Crown offices. A little more time had gone to looking up Henderson's home address. I had walked straight over and I had done the walk at a brisk clip with no loitering along the way, but I had every reason to believe that Dryden had taken it on the run and yet he'd arrived only just before me. It looked like the better part of at least twenty minutes not accounted for.

Could it be that Dryden had done as he said he was going to do? Had he hurried home in the hope of finding that his choan had turned up and would still be waiting for him? Finding that she'd been and gone, had he then decided that since in any case his night was to be a washout, he had time to do a bit of worrying about his boss? Could I believe that this was all there had been to fill the time gap? I tried it on and found that belief didn't come easily.

Upstairs I quickly stopped even trying to believe. The porter ran me up to Henderson's floor and waited with me while I worked on the doorbell. I rang and waited. I could hear the bell, but it was all I heard. No other sound came through the apartment door, no rustle of anyone moving around inside, no footsteps, nothing. I hit the bell again and again I waited.

The porter scowled and scratched his head. "He's in there," he said. "I only just took him up and he hasn't come down again."

"There's nothing wrong with the bell," I said. "I can hear the ringing."

"Yeah. They're loud bells. You can't help hearing those bells anywhere in the apartment."

"You have a key?" I asked.

"The master key."

It was the answer to the question I'd asked and it was all he was giving me, the bare answer. He wasn't bringing out the master key. He wasn't offering to put it to use.

"You'll have to let me in," I said.

He didn't know. Dryden was all right. Dryden had his key. All the help in the house had been briefed on that. Dryden was to come or go unchallenged any time of the day or night. They had orders on that, Mr. Henderson's orders. The porter didn't know about letting anybody else in.

"District Attorney's office," I said, just as a reminder.

"Don't you have to have a warrant or something?" he asked.

He had his own reminders to offer.

I didn't want to go into that. I tried a bit of explanation. I told him there had been trouble over at Henderson's office. I added that I didn't always go around looking the way I was that night.

"If you want some idea of the kind of trouble it's been," I said, "just take a look at me. I came around here on the chance that the trouble wasn't only over at Mr. Henderson's office but here as well. Henderson may be in there needing help and Dryden can have walked into something also. The two of them can be needing help."

That porter was a man of few words. He didn't stop to kick it around. He asked for no details. I made my point and I didn't have to elaborate. With one hand he brought out the master key. With the other he lifted out of its socket the lever handle which operated the elevator.

Taking the handle with him did, of course, render the car inoperative. Nobody could sneak in and run himself to the lobby while the porter's back was turned. If such was his idea, however, it was only part of his idea. The way he hefted that handle and adjusted his grip on it made it obvious that the thing could be put to a second purpose. It was a good, solid, heavy hunk of metal nicely balanced and as comfortable to a man's hand as any weapon. If it should be that Ralph Henderson and/or his secretary needed help, the porter, for one, was going into the apartment at the ready.

Working the key, he swung the door open. It was one of those layouts that has no entrance hall. The door opened directly on a large living room. The room was fully lighted and it stank of stale tobacco smoke. It was a handsome room, solid and comfortable and unpretentious. It was the room of a man who did himself well but without any fancy ideas. It was a room that was pleasant to look at but that in its every detail told you that it wasn't there to be looked at. It was there to be used. At the moment, however, nobody was using it. There was no one in it, not Henderson, not Dryden, not anybody.

We pushed on to do a quick run-through on the rest of the apartment. There was a bedroom, a dressing room and bath combination, a small kitchen, several good closets, and a terrace. Lights were on in every one of the rooms. Even the terrace was lighted, but that was all, nothing else to indicate that anyone had been there that night. Even the stale tobacco stench was limited to the living room. The air in the rest of the apartment was clean and fresh. Everything was in order all through the place. Nothing anywhere could possibly have been interpreted as a sign of struggle.

The kitchen had a service door. I opened it and stepped out to the little back hall that gave access to the fire stairs. There was no one out there. I waited out in the service hall and I was completely still as I listened. If anyone was running down the service stairs, he couldn't possibly be moving so silently that some sound of his movement wouldn't carry back up the stairwell. I know the acoustical properties of the fire towers in buildings of that sort. Put a mouse on the stairs even ten stories away and, if he so much as twitches his whiskers, you're going to hear the rustle of them. I heard nothing.

I returned to the apartment and shut the door after me.

"Dryden is on his way out," I said. "Any way he can leave the building except by the front door?"

"Not this time of night. Service entrance is locked up tight."

"Good. If you take the elevator down, you'll beat him to the lobby. I want you to bring him back up here. Tell him it's my orders."

I expected I'd have to add some persuasion to that, but this was a no-nonsense porter.

"I'll bring him back up here," he said, and he was off.

I admired the way the man said it and the way he moved. He was all purpose and no truculence. There was a job to be done. He accepted the necessity of it and he was going to do it.

Meanwhile I returned to the living room. It was the only part of the apartment that showed any indication of having been in use that night. Someone had been in there smoking heavily. Taking the time now for a closer look, I checked the ashtrays. I have rarely seen so many dead butts. Even the most careless of heavy smokers, coming to a time when his ashtrays are so full that for want of any clear space in them he is tamping out one smoke in the discarded butt of another, will usually go to the little trouble involved in dumping the butts to start afresh with an empty ashtray.

The ashtrays in that room looked as though they hadn't been cleared even once all that night. I made no exact count, but they were heaped with the remains of at least two packs of cigarettes. I could see no lipstick smears. There seemed to be no indication of wet smoking and all the butts seemed to be from the same brand. I couldn't go so far as to conclude that all the smoking had been done by one person. We can leave it that the evidence gave no indication that there had been more than one.

It did, however, give every indication of nervous smoking. Some of the butts had been smoked down so short that I wondered how anyone could have held them without burning his fingers or could have drawn those last drags out of them without scorching his lips. Others were almost full length, looking as though they could have been held only long enough for lighting them and immediately tamping them out.

There was no way of telling how recently all this frantic smoking had been done. In that direction the stale tobacco smoke that hung in the air signified only that the room had not been aired. All the dead butts left lying about could account for much of the reek. Dryden had been there, of course, but if he had done any of this smoking, he could account for only a butt or two. He hadn't been in there long enough for more than that.

I was waiting for the porter to bring him back up to me. This time I was going to shake some answers out of that young man. Unless I could make him tell me what had brought him to Henderson's apartment and why he had been so unwilling to be found there that he'd tried to make his getaway by the back door while I was ringing at the front, it seemed to me that I would be stopped cold on the whole thing.

Ashtrays all over the room were heavily loaded, but the one that was piled the highest was on the desk. The desk top furthermore showed several smears of scattered ash. It was easy enough to picture it. It had to be a nervous man. He'd been cooped up in that room for a considerable time while he'd been sitting something out. Waiting for something?

He had done a lot of floor pacing. The discards of his smoking were all over the room, and between one ashtray and the next I could see on the carpet the marks of dropped ash. If it had been a sloppy room or a disordered room, none of this could have been so obvious, but in every other respect it was one of those rooms that had a place for everything and everything in its place. If it had been a woman's room, you could have immediately known her for a fussy housekeeper. Since it was a man's room, it had a military look. You could imagine the owner standing inspection in it.

There were, however, the cigarette butts and the cigarette ash. If they were Ralph Henderson's they bespoke a night through which the man had been anything but himself. If they were a visitor's, then for some considerable time Henderson's living room had been occupied by a man too distrait to notice what he was doing to his host's beautifully ordered quarters or too hostile to care.

I tried picturing the smoker. I saw him as he paced the floor. I saw him as he settled himself again and again at the desk, anchoring himself there till his nerves again pulled him to his feet and set him to pacing the floor once more.

I put myself at the desk, hoping I might visualize what the man might have been doing there. The desk top wasn't an empty expanse. It held the heavily loaded ashtray, a telephone, a cigarette lighter, the usual pen and pencil in ornamental stand, the usual desk blotter. That, however, was all. No papers, not even a memo pad, only the ashtray, the noncommittal desk furniture, and the smudges of ash across the blotter.

I was staring at those smudges of cigarette ash but only for want of anything else to concentrate on while I was trying to think. Certainly I didn't expect them to tell me anything, and when they did begin communicating something, my bending for a closer examination of them was only idle. I wasn't expecting anything.

One spot of ash on the blotter wasn't evenly distributed. It showed loops and squiggles as though someone had been doodling with the point of a stylus in the smudge of ash. On closer examination I recognized the loops and squiggles for what they were. A sheet of paper set down on the blotter with some of the dropped cigarette ash trapped under it had spread the ash smoothly over the blotter. Writing done with a heavy hand on that same paper had carried through to the ash underneath and left its marks.

What was visible seemed to be not enough to read, only enough to be recognizable as writing. There was, however, something I might be able to do about that. Lifting the lamp off the desk and holding it down at desk-top level, I had the light sweeping across the blotter, parallel to its surface, instead of shining down on it perpendicularly. It worked. I got what I wanted.

The writing had been heavy enough so that it didn't make its mark only in the smudged ash. It had pressed an impression into the surface of the blotter. Shining the light across it as I was, I was bringing up a light and shadow contrast between surface and indentations. It was enough. I had something there I could read.

2 A.M.
linc c
band sh
n side

It wasn't much. My first thought was that I had only a fragment. The hand pressure of the writing had been uneven, and on only this much had the weight come down heavily enough to leave a depression. I jiggled the lamp, working it up and down and from side to side in the hope of hitting a better angle and bringing up more of the writing. It was no good. There was no more.

For a moment I dithered futilely, cursing at the luck that brought me no more than this fragment, but then it came to me that this might have been all there was. That first thought of mine—that lines trailed out and in, disappearing where the pressure lightened—seemed good only until I began examining it.

It was the closing line that first made me question it. If there was any indication of something missing from that one, it would be at the beginning. I could supply a missing letter there and make it read "in side," but it would be just that, the two words. It couldn't be "inside." Since, however, the other lines indicated something missing from the line endings, one could suppose a writing pressure that on each line grew and diminished so that there would have been stuff at both the beginning and end of each line that hadn't come through.

I toyed with possibilities such as "in side door" or "on side wall," but I wasn't convinced. My attention slipped off to the second of the four lines. Everywhere else I could work out reasonable possibilities in terms of prefixing and suffixing to the lines. Line 2 was intractable to this treatment. No prefix in the English language was going to make "linc" a recognizable word ending. "Linc" had to be an abbreviation, just the sort of improvised shorthand we all of us are prone to invent when making quick jottings that need not be remembered for long.

Once I'd seen that, the rest came along quickly in its train. My notions of rise and fall of pressure were completely off base. All the other verbal bits and pieces would be improvised abbreviations just as was "linc." I didn't stop for any further looking at it. I had no doubt that I was making a correct reading and a complete reading. Glancing at my watch, I moved toward the door.

I was cursing the whole succession of small futilities that had eaten up my time. It had been a moment of fruitless delay here and another there, and all those moments could be added up to just the full ten minutes or quarter of an hour which I at that moment needed and which I didn't have.

My watch stood at eight minutes to two and I was twenty-odd blocks away from the bandshell of which I was only vaguely aware. As I recalled it, it stood at the western edge of Lincoln Center, west of the State Theater and south of the Metropolitan Opera House. North side of that would be somewhere along the south wall of the opera house.

Eight minutes to go and I was more than twenty blocks away from where I was convinced I had to be. I could never make it up there by two. At best I was going to be a few minutes late. I was thinking of the way I'd been put out of action and all the measures that had been taken to hold me out of action, and it seemed to me that by just these few minutes those measures were going to be successful. If I had not worked myself free at all I could have done no worse.

Even a few minutes more and I could have allowed myself to take time out for putting in the police call that would have saturated Lincoln Center with men from the local precinct, but by the time I could get over to them what and whom they should be seeking, it would be past the time for them as well as for me. I can't say I knew too much of what I should be looking for, but I did expect that at least I would be in a position to recognize it when I saw it. If in the few minutes available anyone was to try to hit that bandshell usefully, it was going to have to be me.

If it could have been me with police reinforcements, I would have liked it better; but, since it could be only one or the other, I at least did have some small clues to what was going on. Local precinct police would have nothing and there wasn't the time for filling them in even briefly.

I blasted out of the apartment and threw all of my weight against the elevator bell and I kept it there, leaning against the bell. If I had stopped to think about it, I did, of course, know that electric bells either ring or don't ring. Extra weight thrown into pressing the button puts no extra zing in the sound, but I was impatient and I had other things on my mind.

On the ride back down to the lobby I planned to snap out a few orders for the porter. I could do that without any loss of time. He would phone the precinct for me and that way at Lincoln Center I'd have some police reinforcements to go in with me without myself taking even a moment for the call. I did have the thought that alternatively I could ask Dryden to make the call for me, but the thought just came and went. I wasn't giving it any skull room. Dryden had some explaining to do. He was nobody I could look to for cooperation.

Waiting for the elevator to come up, I wasn't too certain that I could rely on the porter either. It wasn't that he was keeping me waiting. Almost immediately on hitting his call button I heard the whine of the air through the shaft as the car began its ascent. What, however, had become of those instructions I had given him earlier? It wasn't as though he had taken them with any reluctance or even hesitation. He had gone off showing every evidence of eagerness to tackle the job of nabbing Dryden for me and bringing him back up to the apartment. I was asking myself what had been going on between them since. Had Dryden proved to be more than the man could handle? After all, if it came to that, could I expect that the man would have used force? It could be that it had been too much to expect of the man that he should come right back up dragging Dryden behind him, but I felt that it shouldn't have been too much to expect that the man would at least come back and report to me.

When the car came up and the door opened, the porter was alone. He gave no sign of its even entering his mind that I might want to be taken down. He was now prepared to give me his report, and he was too full of it to be stopped.

"Mr. Henderson's going to hear about this," he stormed. "I'm not taking the responsibility. Mr. Henderson can take it up with the boss if he wants. He can get me fired if he wants. I'm not going to be held responsible."

I pushed past him into the elevator and past his raging harangue I pushed in the few words it took to tell him I wanted to be taken down to the lobby and without delay. That much he did take in. I had to be away from there and in a hurry, but he was too full of himself and his responsibilities to comprehend any more than that. I wanted to tell him about the call he could make for me, but we had only bare moments together before we were down to the lobby and they weren't nearly enough for shutting him up and capturing his attention.

Guarding the building's front door through the night was his job. He had to keep the door locked and he was authorized to leave it only for such short spots of service as tenants might require during the late hours. Essentially only emergencies were to take him away from his post. His orders, furthermore, were to keep the door locked even when he was right there in the building lobby. It most emphatically had to be kept locked any time he had to leave the lobby, no matter how briefly.

So now the unthinkable had happened. While the porter had been upstairs with me, Dryden had unlocked the front door and had gone off, leaving it unlocked and unattended.

"He has to wait till I get back down to let him out," the porter was growling. "It's the rules here. He's supposed to wait for the elevator so I can take him down and let him out and lock up after him. It's no responsibility of mine if he doesn't wait."

"You're sure that's what he did?" I asked. "I would have heard him on the stairs. There wasn't a sound. There was nothing moving on those stairs."

"He's the sneaky one," the porter growled.

Evidently the porter's rage hadn't stopped his thinking. He had already figured out just how Dryden had managed it. There were four apartments to each floor. All four were served by one passenger elevator, available twenty-four hours of the day, and one service elevator, now locked up for the night. There were, however, two fire towers. Each had its fire stairs. Each served two of the apartments on each floor. Both had access to the elevator hall.

When I rang the apartment bell, Dryden had tiptoed back through the apartment and had let himself out the back door. He ran down the service stairs, but only for one flight. He would have had more than enough margin for reaching the floor below in the time it took us to go through Henderson's apartment and come out the other end into the service hall.

Even if we had not stopped to look for him again and again in our passage through the apartment, even if we had gone straight through at top speed, he would still have had time for the one flight and to spare. As it was, we hadn't gone straight through to the service hall. I had checked bedroom and dressing room and bathroom first. I had even checked closets.

It had, nonetheless, been a quick check. I had been out in the service hall in plenty of time to have heard him even in a stealthy descent that might have already been many flights down, but it didn't matter. He had by then been off those stairs for a considerable time.

After only the one flight he had crossed the elevator hall on the floor below Henderson's and there he had nipped into the other fire tower. While I had been bending my ear to the stairwell of Henderson's fire stairs, Dryden had been over where I couldn't hear him. He had been clattering down the remaining flights in the fire tower that served the other pair of apartments.

Assuming that he had been lying doggo somewhere below on the stairs down which he couldn't have moved without my hearing him, we had expected that the porter in his elevator would hit the lobby before Dryden, even at his nimblest, could have made it by the stairs. The assumption, of course, was based on the belief that as long as I was out in the hall listening, I had Dryden frozen into immobility on the stairs.

Since Dryden had been waiting for nothing, the assumption all too obviously was a sour one. Even while I had been listening in the one fire tower he had been clattering down the other stairs. He had easily been out of the building before the porter returned to the lobby and found the street door ajar.

"I know he couldn't lock it," the porter fumed, "but that doesn't mean he had to leave it standing open, like inviting burglars or who knows what just to walk in."

I had indeed seen the porter lock the lobby door after me and I'd seen him check it before he took me upstairs. He didn't have to tell me how the lock worked. From the inside the door could be locked or unlocked with the simple turn of a knob. On the outside, of course, there was no knob. From the outside locking or unlocking it needed a key, and that key Dryden didn't have. Even the tenants didn't have it. They always waited for the night porter to let them in or out.

You may be wondering why, since all the time I had with the man was these few moments in the elevator, I let him go on non-stop with telling me all this. Why didn't I shut him up and give him his instructions on the call I wanted him to make to the police?

When a man is that aroused and he's going full spate, you can't quickly stop his talking, much less draw out of him the attention it would have taken for him to do any useful listening. Also you must remember that I was operating in a situation of which I knew all too little and understood even less. It was a choice, therefore, between trying to tell him what I wanted of him even though I knew full well that I was most unlikely to get that made unless I hung on with him in the lobby giving it time I didn't have and letting him supply me with these snippets of additional information he was pouring out at me. It was, after all, a little more I would know even if it was nothing more I could understand. Could Dryden have hoped the porter wouldn't tell me he'd been in the apartment? That seemed unlikely.

I was more inclined to think that Dryden's mode of departure indicated that here was a young man who had more in mind than simple avoidance or even escape. He had hurried away from me at the Henderson & Crown offices because he'd had things to do and one of those things had been this visit to Henderson's apartment. To pick something up there? To remove from the apartment something he didn't want me to find? Carrying a hope not unlike mine that in the apartment he would find some clue to just what was going on that night?

It was more than possible that in the time he'd had up in the apartment he had seen there what I had seen. It was even possible that he'd had no need for deciphering it from the indentations in the blotter. The original paper could have been lying there for him to find. It might even have been that very same paper that he had gone to the apartment to find and it might have been that paper he felt had to be removed before I might come on it.

Until I had gone that far in my thinking, I had been reading the scribblings as something in the nature of a memo. They did look like notes a man might scribble from something that was coming at him over the telephone, just memory aids for his own use. That, however, was never more than a guess and the scribblings could just as reasonably have been a message left there for Dryden.

Either way, assuming that Dryden picked up the message, he had not been so many minutes before me that he could have had at his disposal any surplus of time. I could certainly argue that Dryden didn't leave the apartment prior to the moment when I rang the bell. That he used the service door and switched from one fire stairs to the other was solid evidence for that. But for me at the apartment's front door, he would have pulled out of the place by the ordinary route. But for me, obviously, the ordinary route would have been the quickest as well.

I could, therefore, make a reasonably close estimate of how much time Dryden had for making it to a two-A.M. rendezvous at Lincoln Center. The best I could hope might be reaching the scene by a few minutes after the hour. Dryden had no more than just those few minutes that I lacked. He was that brief time ahead of me. With all luck and all speed he could have hoped to be at the north side of the bandshell by two o'clock, and he travels fastest who travels alone.

I had my own traveling to do and I was without wheels. All the time the porter was running me down to the lobby and bending my ear, along with all this thinking I was doing about Allen Dryden, I was also speculating on what my chances were worth for picking up a cab. That time of night in that part of town I could lope off and possibly pick up a cruising hackie en route or I could hang on in front of the house looking for the break of a returning resident who might roll up in a cab I could take over.

Luck briefly turned my way and blew me a kiss. Even while the porter was unlocking the door for me and simultaneously demonstrating how, in the haste of his departure, Dryden had left it ajar, that returning resident did pull up in a cab. It wasn't Ralph Henderson. That lucky I wasn't, but I brushed past the porter and jumped for the taxi. The porter was still showing me how an unclosed door looked and was still discoursing on the evil thereof when my luckily acquired cab rolled me away from there. I was on my own. I could hold no expectation of police reinforcements.

I wasn't much worried about it. There had been a stretch where

I'd worked up a concern for Henderson and his safety that began to take on the color of panic. Going to his apartment, I had more than half expected I'd find him there, victim of much the same sort of manhandling as I had taken. I'd been visualizing him as bound and gagged, so tightly secured that he couldn't even knock the telephone instrument off its cradle.

Finding the apartment unoccupied and since it showed no indication of having served as the setting for any sort of violent encounter, I was now swinging from worry to anger. It had come to look as though nobody had been roughed up—that is, nobody but me. I began hating myself for a fool, telling myself that I should have resisted even a brief slip into thinking of Ralph Henderson as a possible victim. People were playing games that night. It looked very much as though Ralph Henderson was one of the players and had been playing at least some of his games on me. How else could I read that on-again, off-again performance he'd put on earlier in the day?

The more I thought about it, the more I felt it was just as well for me to have it the way it was. I needed no reinforcements. All I wanted was to get there in time to catch up with Ralph Henderson and settle my own personal score. I'd been having a bad night and it was his fault. I'd had enough of his nonsense. I was going to know what this was all about. Even if all the rest of it should prove to be legal, the way I'd been handled wasn't. For that, someone was going to have to answer to the law. For the rest of it, Ralph Henderson was going to have to answer to me.

I had a good cabbie and it was the time of night when traffic runs lightest. He made even better time than I'd let myself hope for. It was only barely past two when he set me down at Lincoln Center. It was no fault of his that it left me not nearly close enough to where I wanted to be. For that you can blame the architects or perhaps more justly the pompously grandiose ideas of the Center's founding committee. What with opera house, ballet theater, repertory theater, and a flock of concert halls plus assorted oddments, the place would have been quite big enough without the grand plaza and the colonnaded promenades they tacked on to give it flash.

The cabbie, since at that time of night he had no clues on which to make guesses, had asked me what part of Lincoln Center I wanted. All parts of it would be equally dark and shut down. When I told him the bandshell, that wasn't any good to him. At more suitable hours he'd have fares going to or from opera house, theaters, or concert halls. He would know the best means of access to all of those, but on the bandshell he drew a blank. Outdoor band concerts, after all, are for free. They draw an audience that doesn't spend cab money on them.

"Bandshell?" he asked. "Whereabouts is that?"

Even though band concerts had never been my thing, I told him as best I could.

"At the back of the layout," I said. "West End Avenue side, west of the State Theater, downtown side of the opera house."

I might have done better telling him nothing. Taking description for instruction, he brought me as close as he could come, West End Avenue at the very spot where the semi-dome of the bandshell loomed against the night sky. I paid him off and, dashing for it, I discovered that I was right there and at the same time not there at all. I was confronted with a blank wall, no entrance of any sort on that West End Avenue side.

I ran down to the corner and pushed into the side street hoping for a way in short of doing the full distance around to the other side of the whole complex where, by the grand plaza, I would be coming all the way back again along the inside route.

I did find a shorter way. It was one of those promenades. As I started up it, it came home to me that at this time of night Lincoln Center is not New York's great cradle of culture. It is not the mecca of all sight-seers. It is only a potential disaster area. Once the final curtains have fallen on all its performances, its audiences take off for subway, bus, taxi or limousine. Within a half hour the whole place is shut down and, once the people are gone out of it, its amenities convert into menaces. Populated arcades may be pleasant places in which to loiter. Dark and with the people gone from them, they become secret places in which to lurk. The fountain, a soothingly murmurous background to the hubbub of the passing crowds, becomes in the silence of the night a veil of plashing sound to stand between you and any possibility of your hearing any of the small rustlings of stealthy movements.

It becomes an area where muggers can lie in wait, a place for the carrying out of such transactions that cannot stand the light of day or the possible notice of some casual passer-by. The shadowed spaces that lie silent and, one hopes, empty between the theaters of music and drama and dance develop the potential of quite another sort of theater, the theater of quite another culture, the secret and sinister culture of crime.

Close alongside me on my right rose the side wall of the State Theater. To my left lay an open area studded with small trees and backed by the hollow of the bandshell, a hole of blacker dark in the general darkness, the mouth of what might have been a cave incongruously precise in its geometrical outline. For crossing to the bandshell and coming around it to its north side my shortest and quickest route would have been a diagonal cut through the open space. Since it was an open space, however, it was an exposed space and my one hope was that the meeting north of the bandshell might not have been so brief an encounter that it would not still be in progress.

If I was to put myself into it without giving any forewarning, it seemed necessary that I myself do some lurking in shadows. I went all the way in, therefore, keeping close to the State Theater's wall, hoping to draw what advantage I could from concealing myself in the black shadow it threw.

When I would come to the end of that wall, I would have an open area to cross before I could again hope to lose myself in the shadow cast by the great bulk of the opera house, but I could wait till I'd come to it before I'd have to decide whether or not I needed to cross it. Once I was that far in, I would be in a position to stand cozily tucked in the blackness of shadow and from there try a long look west along the side of the bandshell. On the basis of what I saw then I was going to come to decisions about how I would move next.

Creeping up on this objective as silently as I could, I had my every sense straining to pick up any whisper of talk or rustle of movement that might come at me in the dark. I was straining after the small sounds. I was wondering whether there would be anything at all for me to hear and expecting that, if there would be, it could only be something just barely audible. Maybe it was because I was listening so hard and maybe it was a heightened resonance of arcaded spaces and travertine-surfaced walls, but, when the shots sounded through the night, their report was louder and sharper than any gunfire I could recall previously having heard.

Strange as they sounded to me, there was no mistaking them and no mistaking the direction from which they came. It wasn't an exchange of shots. There was no bouncing of sound back and forth. It was a rapid-fire fusillade. I recognized it for the heavy bark of revolver fire. There was no counting the shots, but it did sound as though someone had pumped at the trigger until the gun was emptied, and it was not my imagination or my expectations that told me the firing was coming from the north side of the bandshell.

This was no longer something to creep up on. Whether there was anything still to be gained from speed I didn't know. Stealth, however, was no longer going to get me anything. That I did know. Leaving the shadow to which I'd been clinging, I took off on the dead run across the open space in front of the bandshell.

Just as I came to the corner of it, not more than a stride away from where I would turn to follow along its north side, I heard the pounding thud of running feet. These were not my own. Mine I'd been hearing ever since I broke away from the shadow of the theater wall. This was someone else, and he was running toward me, coming away from just that location to which I'd been headed, the north side of the bandshell, the place from which had come the fusillade of shots.

8

I PULLED UP SHORT. Flattening against the front of the bandshell, I waited. The man would be coming past me, but that was going to be as far as he would come. I had myself set to stop him. I was going to take him as he came by.

But he didn't come by. It was impossible that he should have seen me. During the moments when I had exposed myself in crossing the open space, he had been around the corner of the bandshell and there he could no more have seen me than I had been able to see him. Also he hadn't been lurking just around the corner of the bandshell to spy me out. He had been in far deeper than that. I knew that much since I had heard him running toward me.

He hadn't seen me. I couldn't believe that he had heard me either. It seemed to me that the man, as he came out of that area between the wall of the bandshell and the side of the opera house, had the choice of turning either north or south to make his getaway. Pure chance made him turn north. The other turn would have taken him past me. But for me, however, in that direction he would have had the quicker escape route.

As soon as I saw him veer to the left, away from where I was waiting for him, I broke back into the open and took off after him.

He had no great lead on me. It looked like not much more than five yards and, as we raced across the front of the opera house, I gained on him slightly. I was certain I was going to have him. Judging by my rate of gain, however, I expected it would be only after a long chase. But that was on the assumption that the man was thoroughly familiar with the area. He wasn't. As soon as he had cleared the front of the opera, he made his mistake. Taking a slight jog to the right, he could have run past the back of Philharmonic Hall and come out into the street to the north of it. Instead he ran straight on. The imposing mass of the big Henry Moore bronze lay ahead of him, but he wasn't seeing the sculpture as an obstacle in his path. It lay that bit to his left and he was thinking he could run past it. Either he didn't know that it rose from the middle of a broad reflecting pool or he had let it slip his mind. He was all but into the pool before he saw the water and then he had to pull up short at the rim.

In just that moment that he was stopped at the edge of the pool, looking to right and left for his way out, I gained a couple of good strides on him. Assuming that he would see that he had only one choice and that it lay to his right, I veered that way to head him off. He didn't see it and, since I had committed myself in that direction, it must have seemed to him that his best chance of getting away from me would be by taking the other direction. He scuttled off to the left, where, hidden in the shadows, lay another obstacle.

I was just that little faster on my feet than he was, but now I had in addition this other advantage over him. I was a sculpture buff and he was not. By fouling himself up with the reflecting pool around the Moore bronze, he had already lost some of the jump he'd had on me. Now he was going to run smack into the big Alexander Calder stabile. It wasn't going to matter whether he dodged around to the right or to the left of that. Either way he was mine to take. To the left he was going to come into nothing but a dead-end corner with the choice of waiting for me to come in on him there or of doubling back behind the Calder for another try at breaking loose to the street on the north.

I had no problems. Veering to the right, I caught up with him just as he hit the Calder. For a man who didn't know it, banging into it in the dark had to be a spectacularly disorienting experience. It is a structure of heavy sheet metal, which through the balance of its barriers and its openings shapes the space it contains.

Colliding with it, he had no way of knowing what it might be made to do, whether for him or against him. He felt the barrier and he felt the opening. Could he slide through it and come out the other side or would he do better to try to dodge around it? There was nothing on which he could base a choice. If he had been feeling of a sculptural representation of some natural object like a human body, he might just possibly have recognized the shape of it by touch and, recognizing it, he would have had some hope of guessing at the nature and extent of the obstacle. Calder's unique shape gave him no clues. It stopped him cold. He stood there trying to feel his way out. I came in on him and pinned him against the sculpture.

Am I making myself sound too brave or even foolhardy? I'd heard gunfire. The man had come running out of the place where I'd heard it. I had every reason to expect that he might still have the gun. I had, however, heard more than the single shot. It had seemed to me that the man pumped at the trigger till the gun was empty and the hammer clicked futilely on an empty chamber. I'd heard that and in the moments since there had been no time for him to reload. If I was taking a gamble, it wasn't a bad gamble.

He didn't move. He neither fought me nor made any try at wriggling free. For only a moment he was sobbing for breath, but then he began talking. Still lacking for breath, he wasn't up to much more than gasping out the words but he did say what he had to say.

"A man," he sobbed. "He's in there. He's been shot. I'm running for a doctor."

I knew the voice.

"Dryden," I growled, tightening my grip on him.

"Mr. District Attorney," he gasped, matching me recognition for recognition. If there was anything to be made of his tone other than breathlessness, it might have been relief. "It's Mr. Henderson in there," he said. "He's been shot."

It could have been a moment for quick decisions among a multiplicity of choices. Go for a doctor? Run back around the opera house to Henderson? Take the chance on Dryden not being the slippery character he gave every evidence of being and turn him loose to go after a doctor while I went to Henderson? I had the options, and I liked none of them. I was happy enough to be taken off the hook.

The mounting wail of a prowl-car siren made my decision for me. Yanking Dryden away from the Calder, without relaxing my grip on him, I marched him back around the opera house. With the police on the scene I would have both reinforcements and communications. A call going out on the prowl-car radio would bring a doctor around in less time than it might take to find a phone booth with a working phone in it.

I said nothing of this to Dryden and, if I hadn't already exhausted my capacity for being astonished by that young man, I might have wondered more at his sudden docility. I was taking him back the way he had come. He could have no doubt of the direction in which I was propelling him and he had to know we were going for no doctor. He didn't argue about it. He didn't complain or try to persuade. It was as though, while even in the process of telling me he was running for a doctor, he had simply forgotten that a doctor was needed. Giving him the benefit of every doubt, I could try and believe that, hearing the police siren, he had zipped into a thought process that matched my own and accordingly recognized how expeditiously the doctor problem would be handled.

At that moment, however, I was not inclined to give him the benefit of any doubt and, when we came around to the south side of the opera house and I was confronted with the body where it lay at the foot of a light post, my ideas about Dryden came down to only two possibilities. Either I'd caught him when he was not running for any doctor but simply trying to make his getaway or else he had been in the grip of a hysteria that blinded him to the all too obvious fact that the way Henderson was a doctor could be no more than a legal formality, not a life-or-death necessity.

Lying in a pool of light, Henderson was quite dead. I'd heard the shots as those of a revolver being emptied. My ears hadn't deceived me. A revolver had been emptied and its every last slug had been emptied into Ralph Henderson. Even before I'd come close up on the body I could see that he was dead and of wounds that for even seconds after their impact could have left no thread of life in the man. Taking Dryden with me, I moved close up on the body. Dryden gave me no trouble. He didn't even try to hang back and, when we ourselves came into the pool of light which ringed the body, I saw something to tell me that the young man had not made his estimate of his late boss's condition on the basis of any distant view. He'd had a really close-up look. How else would Dryden have come by the blood that soaked his shirt cuff?

The blood on his shirt cuff, furthermore, wasn't all I was seeing now that I had him under a light. If before I'd heard him and recognized his voice I'd had a clear glimpse of him instead, I am by no means certain that I would have known him.

Recall what this character looked like when I had last seen him. What sort of T-shirt has a cuff that could be bloodstained? If Dryden was still wearing the tie-dyed job, it was now under the businessman's proper white shirt complete with cuffs and collar and tie. One of the questions I'd been agitating was what Allen Dryden had been doing with the interval of time he'd had between leaving me at the Henderson & Crown offices and turning up only moments in advance of me at the Henderson apartment. This one question had now answered itself. He had used the time for popping around to his own place and changing into business clothes. It wasn't only shirt and tie. It was also the sober business suit and shoes and socks.

The change of clothes, however, was the least of it. If previously I'd been asking what he'd been doing during the intervening time, I was now asking how even a quick-change artist could in so short an interval have managed changes that were so staggeringly extensive. Even in a twenty-four-hour town like New York you're not going to run into many all-night barbershops. I would guess that you'd not find even the one; but, on the other hand, even if done slowly and carefully, is a self-inflicted haircut ever going to look like the work of an expert barber?

But there it was. The curtains of hair were gone. What he had left was shorter than mine, and in the hair-length department even in the notoriously square DA's office I rate as a cube. A couple of inches had come off his sideburns as well. This was quite another Allen Dryden, precisely the clean-cut, efficient-looking article of office furniture I'd been expecting when, to my astonishment, I'd been confronted with the swinger.

So now, with the one question answered, I had two in its place. How had he in so short a time at an hour of the night when he could have had no professional help with it managed this complete transformation and what could have been his reason for pulling off the metamorphosis?

My police reinforcements were now joining us. Putting such questions aside for later consideration, I turned to cope with the more immediate necessities. The cops took over on all the routine. I didn't have to bother with any of that. I left it to them to put in the calls that would bring the meat wagon and the police photographer and all the technical specialists you want at the scene of a homicide. I concentrated on Dryden and the body.

I observed that Henderson, unlike his secretary, had been making no changes. He was dressed exactly as he had been when he'd called on me what was now many hours earlier. He had been sweating then, you may recall, but now he looked as though that sweat might only have been the beginning, as though he had been pouring sweat ever since, stopping only when the bullets put their stop to it and to him. His collar was stained with sweat and the body of his shirt, where it wasn't wet with his blood, was anything but dry. It was all but dripping with his sweat.

I turned from the body to look at Dryden. Right beside me he was standing over the corpse, but he wasn't looking down at it. He had his head turned away, twisting it as far as his neck would take it to avert his eyes from the body and the blood.

"All right, Dryden," I said. "Time to stop kidding around. What do you know about all this?"

He met my question with one of his own.

"He's dead, isn't he?" he groaned. "Mr. Henderson's dead. He's been killed."

Maybe I should have been moved by what had all the sound of a real pain and a genuine grief. Even if you want to be cynical about it and call it a great job of acting, a piece of most effective theater, maybe I should have been moved by it, but the man had not at any time been sufficiently honest with me to establish for himself even some small degree of credibility, and I was in no mood for theater, not even in those cultural precincts.

"Are you telling me or asking me?" I snarled.

Dryden forgot about straining away from any risk of catching another glimpse of the body. He turned to me.

"He was your friend," he said.

"An acquaintance. What was he to you?"

Wincing away from the question, he choked up. His answer came in a strangled voice. It had more than a hint of sob in it.

"Employer," he said. "Friend. Like an older brother—no. It was stronger than that. Like a father. Damn it, I loved the man."

"It didn't do him much good tonight."

I made it brutal. He wasn't going to suck me into going along with his act.

"If I had only known." He was whimpering now. "I made it here in time. I was right here. If I had only known."

He was again straining to avert his face, but now it was to hide from me the tears he had welling out of his eyes.

"What didn't you know that you know now?"

"That there would be shooting, that he was going to be killed."

He turned back to me with the words tumbling out of him. They were pushing so hard to get themselves said that they had driven from his mind any concern he might have had about letting me see him cry. I didn't have to do any probing to draw his story out of him. He was pouring it and, when I broke in with a question, it was only to pin down some detail he was leaving vague. Even these spots of vagueness were nothing if not natural. Vagueness, you must recognize, is not always suspect. In many situations it is unsolicited precision than can awake suspicion.

Out of concern for Henderson, he had rushed over to Henderson's apartment. Finding on Henderson's desk the memo of time and place, he had been even more concerned. Coming upon it, he'd had certainties that hadn't been available to me. He knew at once that Henderson had himself written it. Also the form and the style of abbreviation were typical of the memos Henderson habitually wrote for himself. Nothing about the memo, in fact, was not typical for Henderson except the odd place and the unconventional time.

"The fact that he wrote it and then left it lying on his desk," Dryden explained, "didn't mean a thing. He was always doing that. He remembered. I don't remember things the way he did. When I found it, I picked it up so I could check back with it in case when I got up here I'd get confused."

He went on to explain his avoidance trick on the back stairs, but it was only an explanation. It was not an apology. He was making no excuses. He seemed to feel that at every point in this most peculiar affair he had behaved irreproachably. As he put it, it had become clear to him that something had gone amiss in the affairs of Henderson & Crown and more specifically with Ralph Henderson himself. Henderson, however, had chosen to keep these troubles, whatever they might have been, to himself. Uncharacteristically he had confided nothing to his secretary and friend.

"I didn't know how to read the signals," Dryden said. "He was my boss. If he didn't want me in, I had no business pushing in. But he was also my friend and, if he was in trouble, could I stay out?"

Undecided about what he was to do—proceed as secretary or proceed as friend—he had been feeling his way. If there were signals that said Henderson wanted him out of it, it seemed to him that there were even stronger signals that Henderson wanted me out of it. He had only just found the memo when I caught up with him at the apartment and, hearing me at the door, he had done what out of loyalty to Ralph Henderson he thought he had to do.

He pocketed the memo and left by the service door, planning nothing more at Lincoln Center than a cautious, exploratory approach with a view toward standing by without even making his presence known unless he came to feel that Henderson needed him so badly that a secretary's tact would necessarily be canceled out by a friend's concern.

So now he was reproaching himself bitterly for the caution of his exploratory approach. In his caution he had taken just that minute or two longer for it and the minute or two could have made all the difference.

It was all reasonable enough. It supplied many of the answers, but not all of them. The most important answers were missing and I was by no means certain that the omissions were anything but conscious and careful. The words just then were coming out of Allen Dryden in spate and he was giving the strongest indications of having opened up completely, but all the same he had me wondering whether all this verbal largess could actually be what he wanted it to appear to be. Was it total candor or an attempt at camouflaging his all-important areas of reticence?

If I knew anything about this character, it should have been that it was just when he seemed the most candid that he bore the closest watching. Caution and tact had held him back just long enough to make him too late to do Ralph Henderson any good. Even that seemed a statement that could be open to question. Accepting it, however, on even the most sympathetic terms, I would still be left with my own knowledge that this young man had not been too late to be at least an eyewitness to the shooting. I had seen him run out of the area immediately after the shots were fired. I hadn't seen him go in.

What he was pouring out at me had every appearance of being a free flow of uncensored babble, but there was nothing in the content of this babble that was as arresting as were its lacunae. Allen Dryden had witnessed the killing and he was saying nothing of what he had seen. I just couldn't make myself believe that this could be an accidental omission. I had to rate it as deliberate and careful.

If he was being careful, so was I. At any point, of course, I could have broken in on him with the obvious questions, but those could wait. For the moment it might be that there was more to be learned from the free choices Dryden was making. I could hope to evaluate what he was telling me in terms of what he was trying to leave out.

Then the questions were answered while they still remained unspoken, and the answers came from the least expected quarter. One of the cops brought me the word. Little more than five minutes had passed since the shooting and, as our report from the scene went zipping in through the PD communications network, it ran head on into a report from a nearby hospital. If the police were interested in the remains of a dead kidnapper, they would find the body lying at the foot of the lamppost just north of the bandshell in Lincoln Center.

The source of this information? The father of the kidnapped child. Having recovered his son, he had rushed the boy to the nearest hospital because obviously enough and naturally enough in the mind of the father the first order of business had been the kidnapped infant's well-being. En route, however, the anguished parent had seen the kidnapper go in to pick up the ransom and in his rage he had paused for just that one moment it took to empty his revolver into the monster. It had been an opportunity he hadn't expected would come his way and, confronted with it, he had found it too gratifying to pass up.

Even in that first report relayed from the hospital there came through what seemed to be a clear picture of the man's state of mind. He was embarrassed and ashamed at having to admit that he had stopped for even that much when, as he was putting it, he should have had thought for nothing but getting the baby to the hospital. He was, however, making no apologies and no excuses and showing not the first concern about what the law might think of his setting himself up as prosecutor, judge, jury, and executioner. In that area he was showing only one worry: Could he expect his wife to recognize that he was only human? What would she think of even a momentary lapse from what she would expect should be his only preoccupation, the safety of their child?

"Any hospital report on the kid's condition?" I asked.

"Sleeping," I was told. "Hospital figures he was drugged to keep him quiet. Anyhow there's nothing there the boy won't sleep off. He's perfectly all right."

"The guys at the hospital giving out any names?" I asked.

Just as a matter of routine, for taking this report from the officer, I had moved away from Allen Dryden. You have a witness and you are going to try to pin him down to what he himself saw and heard. You don't risk confusing him. So far as you can, you keep him isolated from any outside information he might consciously or unconsciously incorporate into his testimony.

This was a time, however, when routine paid off with an extra dividend. We did have identifications, and they were the last names I could have wanted Allen Dryden to hear spoken before we had milked out of him every last thing he might be persuaded to tell us.

The child recovered from the kidnapper was one little Ralphie Crown. His father, who en route to taking the drugged baby to the hospital had paused to empty his revolver into the man he was identifying as his son's kidnapper, was Everett Crown.

In its own crazy way the thing seemed to be beginning to piece together, but only in its own crazy way. Mrs. Crown, so avid on the telephone and so bitterly resentful of all calls that came to her from the police or the DA's office, was no more a mystery. Any mother who is waiting for word of her kidnapped baby and who has heard from the kidnapper those usual warnings against appealing to the police is almost certain to behave as she had done. That was easy.

Turning to thinking about Ralph Henderson, I found no such

simple and ready answers to explain his behavior. I did find glimmerings, ideas that could be developed, alternative possibilities. At that point I didn't try to make even a beginning on thinking them through. They came popping at me, but I set them aside for later consideration.

Everett Crown was at the hospital. Obviously he had a story waiting to be told and his story could be expected to provide the facts for fleshing out many of the matters about which I could now only speculate. Crown had to be questioned. Dryden had to be questioned. The baby might even have a story to tell. That would depend on whether it was truly an infant or a small child old enough to talk.

Answers would be lying all over the place. I had only to go after them. It took no more than a quick huddle with the police officers at the scene to get myself organized. They would take over on Allen Dryden. That lad had a lot to explain. He had been talking much and saying little. The quick-change artist, for instance, was going to have to come up with some very good reasons for his quick changes.

For the moment, however, I wanted to keep the chameleon-type secretary on ice. Armed with every last fact I could hope to elicit from more straightforward witnesses, I would be in a better position for breaking down this slippery character. Holding him till I'd be ready for him presented no problem. The police could let him go on babbling. They could take his statement. They could have him wait while the statement was being transcribed. They could be most careful about the transcript, having him read it again and again before he signed it. There would be no compulsion for them to put their fastest or most accurate typist on the job. A few gross errors could be inserted in the transcript and obviously a man couldn't be asked to sign a document that contained anything he hadn't said. There could be an unfortunate necessity for typing up the whole thing a second time and asking him to do all that careful reading again on the second transcript. Let Dryden talk and tell him nothing. That would be the way they would handle him and meanwhile I could be getting what I needed at the hospital.

Dryden, therefore, was no immediate problem, but another detail popped up and held me a while before I was free to take off to the hospital. The police specialists had arrived. They had done all that was necessary before they removed the body. Lifting it from the pavement, however, they found under it something I had to see.

It was a sizable, paper-wrapped package, a large bundle of money. I hung on long enough to examine it and count it. It was all in tens and twenties and enough of them to make a $50,000 bundle. They were all old bills, not in series. But for the fact that some of them were stained with Henderson's blood, those bills were the perfect reflections of meticulous obedience to a kidnapper's instructions. This would be the way he would want the ransom money.

At the hospital I soon had verification from Everett Crown on that point. Fifty thousand dollars in small bills, old bills, and no recording of serial numbers if they wanted the boy back alive.

"It was the child," Crown said. "Until I had Ralphie back, I wasn't fooling around. I was doing the whole thing exactly as he told me. I was taking no chances on what they could do to Ralphie."

Crown was something of a surprise, but in this deal what wasn't? He wasn't a kid, but he was a lot younger than Ralph Henderson. On looks I was putting him in the early thirties, an impressively young man for even the junior end of the Henderson & Crown partnership. The way he was dressed might have had something to do with the impression he made. Tightly fitted black trousers, a long-sleeved, turtle-necked black jersey, rubber-soled black shoes.

He might have been a fencer seeking to intimidate his opponents by the sable menace of this Stygian appearance or he might have been a war-movie commando accoutered for a night patrol.

It was a theatrical effect, but the drama stopped with the costume. I cannot recall anyone whose manner seemed less self-conscious, more simply natural. He made every sort of polite effort to give me some of his attention, but he couldn't even pretend that his heart was in it. The news that the ransom money had been recovered to the full amount he received languidly. It was a moment when $50,000 was only money. He was still waiting to be told with absolute certainty that his little son was going to be all right.

"Anyhow," he said, "I wasn't thinking about that part of it, but it had to be. I gunned him down when he was picking the money up. I left the rat too dead to go anywhere with it."

"The man you gunned down?" I asked. "Can you identify him? Was it anyone you recognized, anyone you know?"

He stared at me. "You've got to be kidding," he said. "This is a stinking louse who kidnapped Ralphie, drugged him to keep him quiet, and held him for ransom, and you ask is it anybody I know. A guy can have all kinds of friends, but he doesn't have any like that. Of course it was nobody I know."

"Why a friend?" I countered. "A man has acquaintances. He also has people he's just been seeing around. In a crime like kidnapping for ransom, before the kidnapper moves, he usually needs a line on the domestic arrangements of the people. It could have been someone you didn't know but whom you'd recognize from having seen him hanging around the last few days."

Crown shrugged. "Like that?" he murmured. "Could be. I didn't think about that, but, of course, he did know our domestic arrangements and our habits. Now that you speak of it, I guess it did have to be somebody who'd been watching us so he could plan it the way he did."

I worked at drawing from him a coherent chronological account of the whole history: kidnapping, ransom demand, ransom payment, recovery of the kidnapped child, and the error of summary execution that gunned Ralph Henderson down. Since from everything he was saying he had no idea of the identity of the man he had killed and since he seemed to feel that identifying the man could be of interest only to the police and that for him it was a matter about which he could hardly care less, I was careful to tell him nothing.

As it was, the man was sufficiently disorganized. Drawing any sort of coherent story out of him was going to take a lot of doing. I had every reason to expect that once he would learn that, in yielding to his overwhelming rage, he had made that most tragic mistake, a mistake that might well have served as a textbook example of the dangers of bypassing due process, he would fall into a hysteria of remorse and horror that was going to render him useless as a source of any information.

Meanwhile there was nothing that Everett Crown was telling me about the kidnapping that wasn't almost unbelievably routine. If there was anything special about this one, it had to be that it was extraordinarily amateurish. In any kidnapping where the victims have been totally obedient to the kidnapper's injunction against even consulting the police you can expect that their performance will be to a considerable degree amateurish. That you'll find amateurs on the other side of the fence as well is far less likely even though kidnapping is not the sort of crime in which anybody has so long a career that he can, through extended experience, develop any considerable expertise. It is not the technician's crime to the extent that safe-cracking or hotel burglary will be, but it does, nevertheless, have certain basic procedures which should occur to any potential kidnapper. From these only the most arrant of stupid amateurs would deviate.

Judging from Everett Crown's account of events, we were confronted with just such a deviation. This had been an uncommonly trusting kidnapper. He had not waited to have the ransom money securely in his hands before he released the kidnapped child. For all he could have known, he might have been exchanging the child for a parcel of cut-up newspaper. He had also run the risk of losing the ransom through having it snatched away from him at the last moment.

Working at getting his story from Crown, I quickly formed the impression that this last was exactly what had happened. Henderson had moved in with a last-minute attempt to retrieve the ransom once the child was back in his father's arms; and Crown, ignorant of what Henderson was trying to do for him, made his fatal mistake.

There was, furthermore, a considerable body of corroborative evidence to flesh out this picture of what had happened. I was told by Crown that he and his wife had all along been determined to do exactly as the kidnapper ordered. Nothing could convince them that there could have been any safer course to take. They had told no one but Ralph Henderson and Crown's own secretary that the boy had been kidnapped and, although Henderson had wanted to bring in the police, they had made it clear to him that they wouldn't have it.

"I had to keep available for when the kidnapper would get in touch with more instructions," Crown explained, "and somebody had to assemble the ransom money for me and somebody had to stay with my wife. It had to be people I could be sure of, not any know-it-alls who'd go to the cops whether I wanted them to or not. You don't think of it that way until the chips are down, but it's a lucky man who has a friend like Ralph Henderson he can fall back on when the going gets real rough. He thought we should let him talk to the police for us. He has a contact in your office, but when we said no, that was it. He didn't push it. He recognized that it had to be our decision, the boy's mother's and mine, even though he's as devoted to Ralphie as we are. The boy's his godson. It's Ralph, you know. Ralph after Ralph Henderson."

I'd already guessed that much. As I pulled out of him his version of the way the events of the day and night had gone, I could, by piecing together what he was telling me with what I already knew, make several other guesses. The picture shaped itself. We had Crown and his wife determined to go along with the kidnapper's demands even slavishly, seeing no other way that might give them better assurance of the safe return of their kidnapped son. We had Ralph Henderson, senior partner prone when in disagreement with his junior to give the greater weight to his own judgment and experience, godfather almost as desperately concerned for the child's safety as would be the boy's parents, and friend with the true friend's unwillingness to push his own judgment so hard that he might be risking the loss of friendship.

The Crowns didn't want the police in, but their older and wiser friend knew better. He'd had some notion that, presuming on our very slight club acquaintance, he could manage to bring me in and at the same time not bring me in. What else could he have been after when he paid me that visit? He'd been trying to set it up to have me standing by for the ransom payment but only unofficially.

Then, talking again to Everett Crown, Henderson decided that he'd made a bad move. He had presumed too much. The Crowns would never forgive him for bringing me into it, so he'd made the later call in an effort to shut me out. Possibly, if he had been handling things entirely on his own, he would have taken risks the Crowns refused to take. Certainly it appeared as though he had gone through the affair entertaining concerns that the kidnapped child's parents never even considered.

Worried about his partner and friend and hoping that if the opportunity arose he might be able to do something for Everett

Crown that Crown would never try to do for himself, Henderson had gone beyond the services asked of him.

"The rat never contacted me direct," Crown explained. "He contacted Ralph and he gave me all my instructions through Ralph, and Ralph's been great. You'll never know. We could never have gotten through this day if it hadn't been for Ralph. Ralph and Emily. Emily Johnson—she's my secretary—she came over to the house and stayed with Mrs. Crown all evening. When I had to go out to pay the ransom and get Ralphie back, she was with Mrs. Crown, keeping her from going crazy. It's a lucky man has friends like that."

Having tossed this quick commendation in his secretary's direction, he turned back to give me a rapid rundown on everything Henderson had been doing for him since noon, when Henderson came to him and broke the news that he'd had a call from someone telling him that little Ralphie Crown had been kidnapped and that the child was safe and would be well treated as long as everybody behaved and followed the kidnapper's instructions.

The timing at this point was troublesome since Henderson had been to see me well before noon, but Crown was certain of the hour. He couldn't be shaken on it. Noon, neither earlier nor later. Going on with his story, Crown told me that Henderson fixed up the package of ransom money exactly as instructed by the kidnapper and that Henderson stood by, waiting at his telephone till the kidnapper contacted him again and gave him the instructions on the procedure Crown was to follow in handing over the ransom and recovering the child.

The instructions, as Crown repeated them to me, tallied with the memo Dryden picked up off the desk in Henderson's apartment, that same memo that I read from the desk blotter. Following these instructions, Crown said, he deposited the package of ransom money at the appointed time in that passageway to the north of the bandshell and then hurried around into the bandshell to pick up the child.

"I found Ralphie all right," Crown explained. "The kid was there just the way the lousy rat said he would be. He looked okay except that he was asleep and I couldn't rouse him. I grabbed him up and started out of there. I wasn't thinking anything but getting him over here quick so a doctor could look at him and we'd be sure he was all right; but, as I started down out of the bandshell, I heard somebody outside. I looked down over the wall, thinking I'd maybe see the guy and have a description of him I could give the police after I'd had Ralphie checked out. So I saw him. He was just bending down to pick up the package of money, and that was it. I blew. Before I even knew what I was doing, I'd gunned him down. It was only after I'd emptied the gun and I saw him down there with the blood coming out of him that I came to myself. I heard people running down there and it came to me that I'd done a crazy thing. How did I know was he working alone or was it a gang? There I was with the sleeping kid I couldn't wake and an empty gun that wasn't going to be any good to me any more and no telling who was down there and how many of them. I had to get myself and Ralphie out of there and quick. It wasn't only that I shouldn't have stopped for anything before I got Ralphie looked to, but now I'd maybe have to fight our way out of there. I grabbed the kid and I ran south, away from the body and away from where I was hearing the running. But then it was okay. I met nobody, and nobody stopped me. I made it out to my car and I got Ralphie over here all right."

He'd stood by while the child was being examined, but the hospital people took care of phoning the news to the boy's mother.

"She's here," Crown said. "She's sitting with Ralphie, so she'll be there with him when he wakes. I should be in there with them."

"In a minute, Mr. Crown," I said. "There's one thing you

haven't told me. How old is Ralphie? Is he old enough to talk? Can we hope that he may be able to tell us something when he wakes up? Or is he an infant?"

For a moment paternal pride took over from paternal concern.

"Ralphie," Crown boasted, "he's only three, but he's smart. He talks like a grownup."

"Great," I said. "Then we'll want to be there too when he wakes up."

He didn't care for that. "I don't know," he said. "Maybe he's been frightened. We won't want him frightened any more. Any-how it's over. I shot the guy. I took care of that."

"Only if he worked alone," I said, reminding him of a possibility he had himself brought up. "We won't scare the boy. I can promise you that."

"All right," he said grudgingly. "Maybe. It'll depend on what the doctors say and Mrs. Crown will have to agree too. She's a mother. She's been through hell. I don't know whether she'll want anyone coming near him now. You go through a thing like this and it does things to you. She'll never be the same again. I know I won't. Hell. When I think of what I did back there at Lincoln Center, I ask myself was that me? Shooting a man down and then when he's lying there in his blood I go on pumping lead till I've emptied the whole gun into him. If you'd have asked me yesterday, I would have said it was something I could never do. I'd have thought I could never shoot anybody. Now I look back at it and I know I did, but I still can't really believe it. I'm not sorry or anything like that. I'm just wondering at myself. It wasn't me back there with the gun. It was somebody else in my skin, maybe a crazy man and maybe a right guy with more guts than I ever thought I could have. I don't know if she's going to understand how it was or if she'll think I had a mind for the lousy fifty thou when I should have been having a mind for nothing but our Ralphie and if he was really all right. He isn't just my kid. He's our kid, and so far today I've been making all the decisions. It's her turn now. It's got to be just the way she wants it for the boy and nobody interfering with her. She's been great today. You can ask Emily. Emily was with her all through and she can tell you, Mrs. Crown's been great today. She's earned it, so whatever it will be, it has to be the way she'll want it."

He was on his feet making signals that he wanted to be with his wife and his son. It was also obvious that, however rough this thing had so far been on the man, it wasn't over. He had another rough time ahead of him. He was going to have to know who it was he gunned down in that moment when, in his own words, he had been some other man inside his skin. He thought he was beginning to learn to live with that man he had been. What was it going to be like for him when he'd be told just what he did have to learn to live with?

I didn't hold him. I decided that for telling him what he didn't know it would be time enough after Ralphie would wake and we'd have some better idea of just how well the boy had come through the kidnapping experience. As Crown started out of the room to go to his wife and son, however, he stopped for a moment to take care of something he had on his mind.

"I wonder if you'd do me a favor," he said.

"Certainly, if I can."

"It's Ralph Henderson. I asked the people here to call Mrs. Crown and tell her we had Ralphie and he looked to be okay and I asked them to call Ralph. Except for Emily, and she was with Mrs. Crown so she got the news, Ralph Henderson is the only other person who knew and he's as scared and worried as we were. But they've been ringing him and they can't reach him and Emily's been working at it and she's been having no better luck. They've tried the office and they've tried his apartment. Both places they get answers but not Ralph. It's the police, both places, and I can't understand that except that it doesn't matter any more now. Only

Ralph. I can't figure where he can be and he'll want to know. There's Al Dryden—he's Ralph's secretary—and it's always been if I didn't know where to reach Ralph, Dryden would know, but they've been ringing Al's place for me, too, and cripes knows where he is. No answer on his phone. So if you could find any way of reaching Ralph Henderson for me. You know, just to tell him we have the boy and that we're here and how things are with us. I was sure he'd be standing by to get the word. I can't understand it."

9

COME MORNING, the child was awake. He was so patently blithe, happy, and so unaffected by what we'd been thinking of as his ordeal that any opposition to our questioning the boy simply evaporated. In the course of the night the child had slept off a heavy dose of Seconal. According to the doctors, the dose had been neatly calculated, enough to keep the boy in a deep sleep, not so much as could endanger the child. They could not, of course, make any sort of guess on whether so nicely measured a dose had been arrived at accidentally or been based on some expert calculation. Since, however, they estimated it to have been a normal adult sleeping-pill dose, they were inclined to think that only by a happy accident it hadn't been too much for the boy to handle safely.

The Crowns had stayed the night at the hospital, and I was back there early. I had Gibby with me this time. He had been filled in on everything I knew, including my expectation that Mrs. Crown would be giving us a hard time. It wasn't only what Crown had told me. I had vivid memories of the way the lady sounded when I had her on the telephone.

So nothing was as expected. Mrs. Crown also had vivid memories of me on the phone. She was abashed and apologetic. She hoped I would understand. She hoped I would forgive her. Whether it was because she was feeling conciliatory or if it was simple relief at finding her child so completely himself, she welcomed us at the boy's bedside.

He was bright and bouncy, friendly and talkative, and if he had anything to tell us, we just never found the right questions to ask. The child had been in the hands of the kidnapper for a period of about thirteen hours. Since it could be assumed that for most of that time he had been in a Seconal-induced sleep, it was not to be expected that he would have any memories of the drugged hours, but there had to be a time, however brief, before the Seconal would have taken effect.

Reconstruct it for yourself.

Little Ralphie had had his lunch and had been put down in his room for his afternoon nap. Alone in the house with the child, Mrs. Crown, following her daily custom, used the boy's nap time in pursuit of sundry beauty rituals. She did explain them to us but, since we made no effort at understanding them beyond determining that they took time and required privacy and concentration, that's all I can tell you about them. What it amounted to was that the boy was alone in his room for his afternoon nap. Mrs. Crown was within earshot if the child were to cry out, but she wasn't in a position to hear any sounds of stealthy movement in the boy's room or in those parts of the house a kidnapper would have to traverse to get to Ralphie's room and again to get out of the house with the sleeping child.

Gibby broke in with a question.

"Afternoon nap?" he asked. "Does the boy sleep so heavily that he could be picked up and carried out of the house without waking?"

"He's a good sleeper," Crown answered. He was a father always ready to boast that whatever his son did, the boy did well. "We've had him out and it's his bedtime. He corks off in the car on the way home. It's happened lots of times. I carry him into the house and we undress him and tuck him into bed and he never wakes at all. When Ralphie sleeps, he really sleeps."

"At the end of a big day?" Gibby was skeptical. "It's bedtime and a kid has been playing hard all day. They all do that. They go out and it's as though nothing could wake them. But afternoon naps? They're never that tired at afternoon nap time or did you have him at hard labor all morning?"

"Ralphie?" Crown laughed. "This little goof-off. Three years old already and he has yet to put in his first honest day's work."

"It wasn't an ordinary nap," said Mrs. Crown, a humorless woman if I ever met one. "With all that Seconal in him the baby couldn't have wakened for anything." She turned to her husband. "Remember how he was that other time?" she said.

I pounced on that. "What other time?" I snapped. "There wasn't an earlier kidnapping?"

I'd never heard of a case but I wasn't ready to call it impossible. It might have been kidnapping like blackmail. The parents give the kidnapper a demonstration of how easy it can be. They pay the ransom and they knuckle under to the kidnapper's threats to the extent that they don't bring the police into it even after they have recovered the child. So the next time the kidnapper needs an infusion of cash he hits them again.

Does it sound wild to you? It sounded anything but open-and-shut to me, but in its own screwy way it seemed to fit a couple of the case's odder facts. Try as I would, I'd been having trouble with conceiving a kidnapper so trusting that he relinquished control of the child before he had secured the ransom. If this was his second time around with Everett Crown, it seemed possible that the kidnapper, acting against a background of Crown's complete docility, had been lulled into carelessness.

Similarly there was Crown's sudden and to all appearances uncharacteristic fall into hysterical violence. Your baby is kidnapped. The kidnapper threatens to harm the child if you go to the police. Even after the ransom has been paid and the child is back in your hands the threat remains. You are to keep quiet or the kidnapper will be back and he will hit again. You are quiet. You cooperate. He can ask no more of you, but it doesn't save you. He does hit again and you can see nothing ahead but more repeats of the horrible ordeal. You are, nevertheless, still inhibited from doing anything about it because, as things are, you have again recovered your child and there still hangs over you the threat that, unless you keep quiet, there will be still another time and this other time it will be different. Then you see a chance to put an end to it once and for all. You look down at the kidnapper and you empty your gun into him.

Even while I was asking the question and getting my answer, these patterns of events were shaping in my mind. They were beginning to seem so reasonable that when the Crowns both declared that there had not been an earlier kidnapping, I almost wanted to believe they were lying. I've never been a man who gives up happily on the easy answers.

"Earlier kidnapping?" Crown yelped. "What do you think we are? Crazy? A thing like this happens to people once, do they just sit around waiting for it to happen again? You've got to be kidding, man."

"A previous time Ralphie was slugged with a big dose of Seconal," Gibby said. "How did that happen?"

Crown shrugged it off. "That was nothing," he said. "You know how kids are. They get hold of something and, unless you're watching them every second of the day and night, it goes into their mouth. One of those nothing accidents. People with kids have them all the time. You get used to them when you're a parent."

His wife was less philosophical about it. To her a terrifying experience was no less terrifying for not being unique. Even if it was most common, it still scared her.

"Get used to it?" she protested. "Maybe if you're not a mother. That's a scare I'll never forget, much less get used to anything like it. Back when it happened I was ready to swear that there could never be anything that would frighten me the way I was frightened then, but I have learned better. Now there's been yesterday, too, and yesterday was infinitely worse."

"Let's get back to the first scare," Gibby said. "Seconal was left lying around. Ralphie got his hands on it and took one. Whose Seconal was it? Who had been careless with it?"

Crown pushed in to shove Gibby's question aside. It was ancient history. It was the kind of mistake people made only once. They'd had their lesson. That would never happen again. It was no good talking about it.

Mrs. Crown talked. I've noticed that wives are prone to do that. A woman is lucky. She has a husband who readily forgives her faults. He doesn't throw them up to her. He doesn't rub them in on her. Since husband eschews his opportunities to criticize and to blame, wife turns to self-flagellation. Everett Crown could have said that it was her Seconal and that she had been careless with it just as she had been so preoccupied with making herself beautiful that the boy had been snatched right out from under her nose and she never even knew it. He didn't. He even tried to shush her when she spoke up to blame herself.

"It was my Seconal," she said, "and it must have been my carelessness. I have no memory of leaving it out where Ralphie could get at it, but it had to be me. Nobody else would have been handling it and the very fact that I can't remember doing it makes it one of those things that you do so much without thinking that you never even know you've done them."

Briskly Gibby brushed by the guilt feelings.

"It happens to all of us," he said. "The boy got hold of your Seconal and luckily he took only one."

"He got hold of only one," Mrs. Crown explained. "It was the last one in a bottle, so we knew it was only one."

"Great," Gibby muttered. "And from that time on anyone who knew about it had what amounted to a doctor's prescription. One of your Seconals would keep the boy safely asleep without any risk of its being a fatal overdose."

Crown blinked. "You mean it was someone who knew?" he asked.

"Possibility worth exploring," Gibby murmured, keeping it noncommittal.

"But who could know?" Mrs. Crown gasped. "The two of us? The pediatrician?"

"All our friends," Crown added, "all the kids at the office. When it happened, we talked of nothing else. Anybody who'd listen got the full play by play."

Gibby picked it up. "Okay," he said. "It's beginning to fit together. Somebody who knows you. Somebody with whom the boy is at home. Somebody who could pick the child up and carry him away without any struggle or outcry."

Crown laughed that off. "Struggle or outcry?" he said. "The way Ralphie was doped up, there wasn't any worry about struggle or outcry."

"After the Seconal took effect," Gibby argued. "It isn't instantaneous, you know, and you can't believe that the kidnapper sneaked into the house, gave the boy the Seconal, and then waited with him till he was sound asleep before carrying him away. There had to be a period at the beginning when Ralphie was conscious and awake."

He developed it for them and, although it was clear that the ideas he was opening up to them shook both of the Crowns badly, they could find no way of rejecting the implications. Even on the assumption that the boy was napping when the kidnapper came in on him, there would be no way of imagining the kidnapper getting the Seconal into the child without the child waking and in some way reacting to the intruder.

"So there it is," Gibby concluded. "He saw his kidnapper, but it was somebody the boy knows and somebody with whom he's so comfortable that there was no fright in it and no surprise. It was so commonplace that it was an episode the child found not worth remarking and, followed as it was by his long, drugged sleep, he's blacked out on the whole thing—that time before the Seconal took effect along with the time he was under the influence of the drug."

Crown winced. "It makes sense," he said, "but only one kind. It makes head sense but it doesn't make heart sense. Put yourself in my place. Could you imagine one of your good friends doing a thing like that to you?"

Gibby shrugged. "It happens," he said. "If it never happened would the language have a word for it? It's known as betrayal."

"Sure," Crown conceded. "There are people like that, but anyone we know? I can't believe it."

He had himself mentioned the kids at the office and I couldn't but think of Dryden with his slippery movements and mad disguises. Even before this session with the Crowns I'd been having questions about Dryden. Now, as Gibby was lining up detail after detail of what they had to tell us, I found Dryden turning up in the central spot of every picture I could make. I could start it with Henderson. Knowing that something was in the making, worrying about it but not knowing what it was going to be and not able to believe it of his trusted secretary and good friend, Henderson came to me. He wanted me to stand by. He wanted to be prepared but he also wanted to think he was wrong in his suspicions. That was why he wanted to keep it unofficial, leaving me open to move officially only if and when the proof might be in.

He brought me into it and then he tried to shut me out. He told me that he'd learned that his suspicions were groundless, but actually he had learned the exact opposite and he had further learned that the situation was far more dangerous than he had ever anticipated. He pushed me off and I could see that from where he stood everything he did after that seemed to make excellent sense. He had to see that his young namesake was safely returned to his parents, but at the same time he wanted to do whatever he could for Allen Dryden.

The young fellow was his protégé and his friend. When Henderson came to me, he must have been thinking that Dryden had gone wrong and that it might be his painful duty to turn the young fellow over to the law. His worst forebodings, however, had not encompassed anything as grave as kidnapping, and the kidnapping brought him to a complete change of mind.

Henderson was not the man to believe that anyone he had known and liked and trusted could possibly sink that low. There would be only the one way Henderson could have explained Allen Dryden to himself. The young man was sick. The kidnapping had to be an act born out of a sick mind.

So Henderson called me off and Henderson spent the rest of the day working with a double purpose. The first order of business, of course, would have been to recover the child unharmed. He could play it exactly as the frantic parents wanted it played and then, once they had the child back, he could make his try at the rest of his program of mercy. He would do every last thing he could in an effort to save poor Allen Dryden from himself.

I could imagine Dryden phoning the ransom instructions to Henderson. He would have used some sort of disguised voice. I already knew him as a youth with a penchant for visual disguises. There was every reason to expect that he would go for an aural disguise as well and, just as his changes in appearance—wildly extravagant as they were—could fool no one, it seemed obvious that any phony voice he might have put on would have failed similarly of deceiving anyone. Such an attempt at deception would most certainly have failed with Ralph Henderson since Henderson knew Dryden so well.

Henderson, however, had played along. Who wouldn't? You find yourself confronted with a close friend who has gone dangerously mad. You don't go for any showdown. You don't let him know you see through him. You wait your chance, hoping for some moment when you may be able to step in and turn the disastrous affair toward a conclusion that might be happy for everyone.

Relaying the instructions to Crown and giving Crown no hint of the kidnapper's identity or of Henderson's own hope that he might manage to save not only the kidnapped kid but the kidnapper as well, Henderson turned up as the third man at the kidnap rendezvous. He saw Crown leave the ransom money and he saw Crown pick up the child. The moment he had wanted arrived. There was his chance to nip in and make his first move toward saving Allen Dryden from himself.

Getting to the deposited ransom payment before Dryden could —and without his knowing it, I had helped him there since Dryden, forced to cope with me, would have been thrown off, even if only a bit, on his timetable—Henderson would scoop the ransom package up. The point of that move, of course, would have been to erase as much of Dryden's crime as possible. It had been a kidnapping for ransom. Now if the ransom payment could be retrieved before it came into the kidnapper's hands, the kidnapping in actuality, even if not in intent, would be reduced to a lesser crime and Henderson could hope that he might then reason with the insane young man.

I was imagining the words he would have been rehearsing. He would have told Dryden the sad truths about himself. He would have explained to Dryden that he was not a criminal but a sick man. He would have shown him how sick his crime had been. It had not succeeded because there had never been any hope of its succeeding. It had at every turn been too insane, freighted on all sides with every potentiality of disaster and nowhere with any possibility of success.

He would have told the young man that they could all be thankful that this madness had come to so successful an issue. There would be no need to bring the law into it. With the child no worse for his adventure and the ransom payment recovered intact, Henderson could promise Dryden that he would plead Dryden's case with the boy's mother and father. He would guarantee that he would win for the unhappy young man the Crowns' sympathy and understanding. They would all work together and, with nothing now required of Allen Dryden but that he put himself in the hands of a psychiatrist and that he stick with the treatment until pronounced cured, this whole miserable business would be cleaned up decently and humanely.

Ralph Henderson, of course, had reckoned without Everett Crown's all too understandable paroxysm of rage. I was guessing that he hadn't known and had never imagined that Crown would be going armed when he set out to keep the ransom appointment. He had himself gone unarmed and, if anyone should have been carrying a gun to that meeting by the bandshell, I was thinking that it would more naturally have been Henderson. Obviously he wouldn't have wanted a shootout, but certainly Crown should have wanted one even less. No father could have been so stupid that he would have considered adding further peril to the life of his child with such antics, and surely he could have in no way foreseen any possibility that, once the kidnapper by handing over the child had divested himself of that one guarantee any kidnapper has for his own safety—the concern a parent must feel for the safety of his child—any kidnapper was going to be so inept that at this stage of his crime he would expose himself to the wrath of the man he had so gravely injured.

I tried it on the child.

"You know Mr. Dryden?" I asked.

Some of the boy's cheerful bounce went out of him.

"Bad man," he said.

"Bad man lifted you out of your crib yesterday and took you away?"

"Allen?" Mrs. Crown interrupted. "Impossible."

At a look from Gibby she fell silent. I pressed the child.

"Was it bad man Dryden?" I asked. "Bad man Allen?"

"Bad man," the child repeated.

Crown plucked at my sleeve and drew me aside. He wanted to explain. Dryden was just no good at all with children. Little Ralphie disliked the man intensely. If Dryden so much as came near the boy, the child screamed the house down. It could not have been Dryden. That was a certainty.

Mrs. Crown joined us. She made no attempt to conceal her dislike of Dryden, but I could see that the root of her feeling lay in her baby's abhorrence of the man. She was in complete agreement with her husband. Dryden could never have come near the boy without Ralphie raising an outcry that would not only have alerted her. It would have roused the whole neighborhood.

Meanwhile Gibby was talking with the boy, trying to get him to name someone, but the child appeared to have blacked out completely on that period of time before the drug could have taken effect. All Gibby was getting out of him was "Mummy" and "Daddy."

Since this approach all too evidently was getting us nowhere, my thinking switched to another question that had begun haunting me. The more I worked at reconstructing the tragic mixup, the more I felt it to be a question that had to be asked. I was still in the process of framing it in my mind, however, when with that half an ear I had been giving to Gibby's questioning of the child I heard Gibby, as he turned to Everett Crown, launch into the preliminaries that would set Crown up for this very question I'd been shaping for the man.

I waited and let Gibby ask it. First, however, he moved it out of the kid's room, leaving Mrs. Crown with the boy.

"You own the gun and you're properly licensed for it, Mr. Crown?" he said as soon as we had the man alone. "Do you make a habit of carrying it?"

"On me?" Crown answered. "Gosh, no."

"Do much practice firing?" Gibby asked.

"Target shooting," Crown answered. "Not as much as I should do, but what with family and business—both the things that should take precedence and all the other things that somehow creep in—there's never enough time." He took a moment out to think and then another moment to try to tamp down an expression of smug self-satisfaction that had crept up on him. "Considering the way my first shot zeroed in last night and the way the whole load held right on the target, maybe what practice shooting I've been getting in has been enough. It either has to be that or, with the desire there, I was operating way over my head."

He was reluctant to boast, but he was obviously more than pleased with the quality of his marksmanship.

"A hobby that paid off," Gibby said.

I recognized the words for a wry comment but only because I know Gibby well and I know exactly where he stands on the question of the private citizen who takes the law into his own hands. The most he will ever concede is that, given circumstances where the provocation is overwhelming, the act may be understandable. He will never allow that anything short of an immediate necessity for saving a life can make it right. There was nothing, however, that he permitted to show either in his tone or his manner that could have given even the faintest hint of his distaste for the shooting.

"Hobby?" Crown demurred. "I've never made it a hobby. I figured it was something I had to do. Just as I wouldn't think I had a right to own a car unless I was a really good driver, I don't think a man should own a revolver unless he's real good at handling it."

He furnished the complete explanation. Before young Ralph was born they had lived in an apartment. There had been protection, a stalwart screen of building staff always standing between the apartment and any hostilities that might have been prowling the world outside.

"When the boy came," he said, "we wanted more room and a yard for him. The house came on the market. It was a steal. Anyone could see that the way Manhattan real estate was going we weren't going to see one at anything like the price ever again. It's a good house, but a house isn't like an apartment. You have windows down at street level and your door is the street door and nobody out there watching it for you night and day. Maybe there was a time when it didn't make all that difference and maybe we took the house at just the wrong time, but you know how it's been the last few years, the way the crime thing has been growing and growing."

He went through all that stuff you hear all over. Burglaries in houses along his street even though his house hadn't been hit, neighbors taking to arming themselves.

"Everybody was getting guns," he said, "as though that was going to be enough. I know any number of guys. Revolver in the drawer of the bedside table and they've never fired it even once.

If they ever had to use it, they'd be so scared of the bang that they'd keep their hands over their ears while they were trying to squeeze the trigger. It's crazy. Me, as soon as I got the revolver, I started practicing with it. Not as a hobby, though, but just so I'd be competent with it the way I'm competent behind the wheel."

"You're downgrading yourself," Gibby told him. "Last night wasn't mere competence. It was great marksmanship."

Crown shrugged the compliment off. "Lay it to desire," he said. "I'd never be able to come near it again, not in a million years, because I'm never going to be able to hate anybody that much again, not in a million years."

"You said you don't usually carry it on you," Gibby reminded him. "But there have been times when you did?"

"I joined a gun club so I could get the practice," Crown explained. "Going down there for a go at the target range, of course I took it with me."

"Only when you had to take it along for target shooting?" Gibby persisted. "Never otherwise?"

"Never till last night."

"Last night was special?"

Crown gave it a long pause before he answered that question. He studied Gibby for a while and from him he looked to me. He might have been trying to assure himself that Gibby was a unique nut and that he wouldn't be encountering any more like him.

"Look, man," he said, "how many guys do you know who lose their kid and have to go out with a packet of money to buy their baby back from some rat who snatched him and they've had this happen to them so often that it's nothing special? Last night was special all right. Last night was darn-tootin' special."

"Nobody's going to give you an argument on that," Gibby said, "but what gave you the idea you'd have any use for the gun? You couldn't even for a moment have been considering a shootout with young Ralphie in the middle. So you hoped that the kidnapper was going to be so stupid that he would let you get a shot at him after you had retrieved the boy?"

"What's wrong with that?" Crown growled. "It's exactly what did happen, isn't it?"

Eventually, of course, he was going to have to be told that it wasn't exactly what happened, but Gibby wasn't quite ready for that yet.

"What's bugging me," Gibby said, "is how you could possibly have had any thought that it might happen unless you knew the kidnapper and knew him so well that you could predict even his most peculiar behavior."

Crown turned from him in impatience. "There you go again," he said. "What kind of people do you think I know?"

Gibby was ready to tell him. "You killed a man last night and you don't know who he was?"

"I sure do know who he was. He was the rat who kidnapped my baby. That's who he was."

With every appearance of making a switch in subject, Gibby pressed on.

"Last night," he said, "I've been told you were worrying about your partner. You wanted him to know you had the boy back and you had expected he would be standing by to get the word. So you couldn't understand why you weren't able to reach him. Mac says it was bothering you. Have you talked to him since?"

Crown relaxed. It was evident that this was a question he welcomed. He didn't put it into words, but his manner was eloquent enough. He might have been telling Gibby how pleased he was to have come to a place where Gibby was finally ready to switch from asking ridiculous questions and to begin showing some interest in things that really mattered.

"It's crazy," he said. "We just haven't been able to reach him anywhere and it's the same thing with his secretary, a kid named Dryden. It's like the both of them have just dropped off the face of the earth."

"And you haven't seen a morning paper or the TV news?" Gibby asked.

The way Crown first reacted to that question, he had taken it as a return to nonsense and he had run out of patience with all that.

"Newspapers?" he growled. "TV? What am I supposed to be? Some kind of a publicity nut who can't wait to see what kind of a press his kid's kidnapping is getting?" The beginning of that was belligerently resentful, but word by word the feeling drained out of it. He was detectably slipping over into doubt and apprehension. He pulled himself up. He gulped. He braced himself. "Ralph," he said. "I don't mean our Ralph, not the baby. Ralph Henderson? Has something happened to him, something I ought to know, something that was in the news?"

"In the news," Gibby told him, "all over the TV. Ralph Henderson is dead. He was shot last night. Enough slugs in him to have wiped out a whole gang of kidnappers."

Crown dropped into a chair and buried his head in his hands. For a while he just sat there shaking and when he pulled together enough to speak, even then it was without raising his head. He babbled wildly from behind his hands. It seemed to me that if I had taken it on myself, I might have found a less brutal way of breaking it to the man, but as soon as I tried to find the words I might have used, I could think of none that would have been any kinder. What sweetener can you put in the message when you're telling a man that he made a little mistake and slaughtered his best friend?

"Ralph?" he moaned. "But why Ralph? Because of what I did to them? Getting at me through Ralph? Holding him responsible for what I did to their man because the arrangements were all made through Ralph?"

"He got it in the passageway between the bandshell and the opera house," Gibby said.

"In the same place," Crown gasped. "They brought him there and did it to him in the same place. They were taking no chances I wouldn't know what it was for."

"It was quicker than that," Gibby said. "He was right there. Nobody brought him. He died with the ransom money in his hand."

Crown brought his head up out of his hands. He was white-faced and wild-eyed.

"No," he screamed, with the scream dying away quickly under the soundproofing of the hospital corridor. Startled, nevertheless, by the volume of the sound that shock had wrenched out of him, he lowered his voice. "No," he whimpered. "You mean me? You mean I? That was Ralph? What did he want to come in and mess with it? For the money? Just for the lousy money?"

As he repeated the word "money," even the whimper faded out and, watching the man, you could see a change come over the quality of his grief and horror. He brought his arms together in front of him and grabbed hard at his elbows, pressing his forearms tight against his gut the way a man will when he has the feeling that he must hang on frantically because he is coming apart.

"Ralph," he moaned. "Why Ralph? I knew. I've known for a long time. I wasn't saying anything. I was leaving it to you to work it out and even if you didn't, was it going to matter between you and me, Ralph? I kept hoping that you'd maybe even tell me and we could have worked it out together, you and me. But this way, Ralph? It didn't have to be this way, old friend, old friend."

The tears had welled up in his eyes. They were spilling down over his face. He was ignoring them. It no more bothered him that we were there seeing him cry than that we were there hearing him talk to his dead friend and partner. It seemed to me that he had forgotten us. He no longer knew we were there.

Gibby reminded him. "Work what out?" he asked.

Coming out of his private agony with a start, he pulled himself together. He hauled out a handkerchief, mopped his tears, and blew his nose. When he emerged from behind the handkerchief, he was another man—still ravaged but hard-faced now and ready to cope.

"Any other way," he said, "it would have been me to see about the funeral and all. We were as much family as Ralph had, my wife, the boy and me. He had nobody of his own. The way it is, though, I guess it had better be Allen Dryden if you can find him. He was close to Ralph, too. You're going to have to tell me what I must do now."

"Allen Dryden," Gibby said. "What can you tell us about Dryden?"

There was still his previous question standing unanswered, but nothing could have been more obvious than that Crown had slammed shut the door he had briefly allowed to swing open. Before Gibby could profitably repeat his "work what out," he was going to have to do some sneaking up on it.

"Allen," Crown said, and if he was trying to dissemble the relief he was feeling at Gibby's not pursuing the other question, it seemed to me that he was doing a miserable job of pretending. "Allen Dryden," he said, "is a brilliant boy, a comer if I've ever seen one. Brilliant and devoted. He was absolutely attached to Ralph. Allen worshipped him. The sun rose and set in Ralph. With Allen's ability he should have moved up and on. He should have left us a long time ago. He was much too good a man for any secretary job. He's been wasting himself with us and, even though Ralph would have missed him like sin, Ralph did try again and again to shake him loose. It was for Allen's own sake, of course, but he couldn't have driven Allen away with a ball bat." Pausing a moment, Crown winced. The pain was hitting him afresh. "Now, of course," he said, "there'll be nothing to hold Allen any more.

He won't be staying with us long. Nobody and nothing to hold him now except wanting to kill me. He will want to kill me, but he'll only want to. He won't do it. He's too smart, smart enough to know he'd be doing me a favor and Allen Dryden won't be doing me any favors."

"That sharp and that close to Henderson," Gibby murmured. "He should have the whole story on what it was you and Henderson could have worked out."

If there was ever an effortful look of bafflement, the look Everett Crown turned on Gibby was it. It seemed to be trying to say that he hadn't the faintest notion of what Gibby was driving at. Actually it was saying that he wished he could have no idea of what Gibby was after and that he wished even more fervently that he'd had the control it might have taken to have kept a securely zipped lip.

Holding him under a steady gaze, Gibby was watching the man work at it. Crown flinched away from Gibby's eye, but Gibby wasn't letting him off the hook.

"The story will come better from you, Mr. Crown," he said. "Getting it from Dryden, a jury might easily become confused about your motives. It could be a confusion that would even have them thinking in terms of first-degree murder."

Crown sneered at the suggestion. "Intentional, planned, with malice aforethought," he said, "for a lousy fifty thou? You should have come up with that one on a day when I was more fit for laughing. Ralph Henderson was my friend and, no matter what, no man ever had a better friend. So now Ralph is dead and I killed him. I have that to live with the rest of my life. I made a terrible mistake and it's going to be with me always. It's enough and now I'm going to leave it that way. I'm not going to do to him dead what I'd have never done to him alive. Ralph's going to his grave a decent man because he was a decent man. He was the most decent of men and I'm not going to be the one to do anything to change that."

"It's not that easy," Gibby said. "Your boy was kidnapped. The kidnapping was done by someone who could get into your house, somebody who knew the boy's nap time and who knew the room where the boy would be sleeping. It was someone the boy knew."

"We've been over all that," Crown mumbled.

"And we still have to find the kidnapper," Gibby pushed on over the interruption. "In looking for him, we're going to have to poke into every aspect of the kidnapping. Those aspects include the strongest evidence of an inside job, and I don't mean only inside your home and inside the circle of people who know you well. It's also inside your business." He turned to me. "Fill him in, Mac," he said. "Tell him your part of the story, Henderson yesterday and the Henderson and Crown offices last night."

I gave Crown the whole rundown, but I kept it strictly objective. There were still all those questions I had about Allen Dryden. I brought none of those into it, but I omitted none of the facts and the facts inevitably included Dryden's quick changes, Dryden's slippery moves, and the reception I walked into when I opened the front door to the Henderson & Crown offices.

I would have said no man could ever be more crushed than Everett Crown had been before I began telling him all of this, but I would have been wrong. As I went through it, I could only think that I was adding a fresh burden of grief to the insupportable load the man was already carrying. He waited till I'd told it all and even then he said nothing, leaving his look of abject misery to speak for him.

Gibby waited for the man to say something. When he remained silent, Gibby prodded.

"It just won't cover up, Mr. Crown," he said. "So?"

"Ralph turned to Dryden," Crown said, and now there was bitterness in his tone along with the pain. "He trusted Dryden when he should have trusted me. I never thought he would do that but I suppose it was because it wasn't Dryden's money." Shaking himself, he took a long breath. "It hurts," he said, "but it can't make any difference. I can see that you'll have to probe it and I know what's going to happen. You'll bring the whole thing out, the complete mess in all its nastiness and there isn't a thing I can do to stop you, but don't look for any help from me. He was my friend. Even if it's turning out that he didn't feel about me the way I felt about him, that can't change the way I felt about him and the way I shall always feel about him. I have killed the man I loved best in this world. That's enough. It's agonizingly more than enough. I'm not going to louse his memory up as well."

And that was it. Everett Crown was saying no more.

10

ALLEN DRYDEN, however, although hardly more inclined to talk, did eventually respond, if not to pressure, at least to persuasion. From the outset, so long as it was a matter of telling us only about himself, he gave it every appearance of the open-book treatment. It was only when the questions shifted to the affairs of his late employer and beloved friend that he showed any symptoms of clamming up. In this area it took time and effort to break him down and, when ultimately he was persuaded to speak, what he had to tell us had to be drawn out of him, and at no point did he make any secret of the pain he suffered under the extraction.

On his own movements and behavior of the night before he appeared to be astonished that anything he had done could be found so much as questionable. That he might to any degree appear suspect never seemed to have occurred to him and even after, from the trend of our questioning, he recognized that he was under suspicion, it was still no sweat. His every answer was quick and offered with complete assurance. It was odd of us to be questioning him at all, but there was nothing he couldn't explain and most glibly to boot.

The quick-change deal, for example, was indeed quick but it had been carried off well within the margins of the most ordinary human capacity. It was by no means the lightning-quick operation that I had visualized.

"I had to change," he said. "It doesn't take a lot of time either way, but the with-it-to-straight change is a lot faster than making the switch in the other direction."

"What do you call not a lot of time?" I asked. "Obviously getting it cut and having a shave will be a lot quicker than growing it out, but no matter how fast you sprout it, bringing hair and beard to the lengths you had them is no matter of minutes or even hours. It's not even days or weeks. You'd have to give it months."

The look he turned on me was pitying. "You didn't think any of that was for real?" he asked.

"We're not finding it easy to think that you're for real," Gibby said, answering for me. "You're going to have to convince us."

Dryden shrugged. "When you're out for choan," he asked, "how do you dress? The same way as you dress for the office? It was going to be a night I would have to myself, private-affairs stuff. I made myself look good. For the office I make myself look businesslike. Do you always look the same?"

"If choan is what I think it is," Gibby said, "of course there's a difference, but it isn't clothes or hair."

"Girls," Dryden said. "Dames, chicks, babes, birds, tomatoes." He gave it the thesaurus treatment rather than attempting to zero in on whichever antiquated term it might be that we'd have in our vocabularies.

"We gathered as much," I told him.

He seemed gratified at having that understood and went on to put us right on the rest of it. Choan, he insisted, are congenitally clothes-conscious. What a man wore did make a difference, but if you really wanted them to tune in to you, you had to have hair. Head hair and facial hair, it was all big with choan.

He explained that there were some businesses where the barriers had fallen but that unfortunately the Henderson & Crown offices were not of their number.

"It's a strong and solid operation," he said, "and maybe it does need the kind of image it's always maintained. You know, reliable rather than daring. I think they would lose nothing by loosening up. They might even gain, but it's never been for me to say. The only thing that ever kept me there was the way I felt about Ralph Henderson. There was a man to work for. I could never walk out on that." He sighed and he pushed back the pain till it was again showing only in his eyes and the set of his lips. "Now that he's gone, I'll be moving—some outfit that's more my style."

"Tell us about your style," Gibby said. "Let us have a little detail on the quick change. We need the hows and whys."

He explained. It was a complicated life. He had a newly acquired girl and she was no ordinary girl. She was his dream choan stepped out into waking life, but still there wasn't much smooth running in his path of love. He had scheduling difficulties. He was in business. She was an actress. During her free time he was tied to the office. Evenings when he was loose and ready for love, she was occupied behind the footlights.

"She could wake up in time to catch lunch with me," he explained, "but I've never pushed for that. The thing isn't solid enough yet for me to let her see me when I'm wearing my office look, so it's got to be only Sundays and nights after the show." He turned to me. "I was waiting for her when you called me last night."

Because my call sounded urgent and because he'd expected he would be quickly finished with me and could then return to his rendezvous, he had nipped over without converting to his office look. As you have probably guessed by now, the flowing locks were a wig and the sideburns were pasties even though he did insist that they represented the true him while his shaven and shorn office image was, in fact, the disguise.

"But once I came over," he said, "it looked like Mr. Henderson was in trouble and that knocked out any plans I'd been having for the night. I had to get loose from you so I could nip home, change over to my office look, and get with it to see what maybe I could do to help Mr. Henderson."

"You had to get loose," Gibby echoed. "You had to shuck out of the fly vines, and the rug, and the bush. Why did you have to? Mac had already seen you as you really are. Whom were you expecting to fool?"

"Nobody. I needed freedom to operate. I had to get up to Mr. Henderson's apartment. He hadn't been answering his phone, so either he was out or, if there, he would have been in no shape to let me in. I had my key to his place. I always had a key, so that was no sweat. The trouble was the night man on the door over at Mr. Henderson's place. He knows me and he'll let me go up any time, but not the real me. He knows me only in my office look. I had to make the change to get past him."

"Okay, and what made you go to all lengths to shake Mac? You'll have to explain that."

He explained it. "I've been Mr. Henderson's secretary," he said. "We were never so pompous that we called me a confidential secretary but that was actually what I was. Even in ordinary matters, if Mr. Henderson wanted anything known, he gave it out. It's never been any part of my job to open anything up and it always was part of my job to know without being told what was to be private and what public. So here was something Mr. Henderson was involved in and it was rough. It was also private. It was so private that even I didn't know anything about it. If he hadn't seen fit to allow me any knowledge of it, what gave me any license to think he'd want me opening anything up to you? The way I saw it, my job was to try to find him and to stand by ready to give him any help I could, and helping him obviously would include giving him every possible assist toward keeping private what he wanted private."

And that was it. In Henderson's apartment he had found Henderson's memo. That had been easier for him. He'd had the actual writing, no need to decipher anything from depressions in the desk blotter. He still had the memo and he turned it over to us. I wondered whether we could have picked it up so easily if it had contained anything he could have thought we didn't already know.

The rest was as I'd had it from him the night before when I picked him up in rapid retreat from the scene of the shooting. He did admit that, in spite of the act he'd put on for me, he'd known from the first that Henderson was dead. He heard the shots and he saw Henderson fall. He ran to him, hoping he might be able to help the man, but as soon as he touched Henderson's body he had known that his employer and friend was already dead.

"Then what was the doctor for?" Gibby asked. "You tried to break away because you were in one great hurry to get a doctor."

Dryden shrugged. "Would you expect that to have been one of my more rational moments?" he asked. "Okay. I've just seen my best friend shot down in front of my very eyes. So I lost my cool. So for a while there I wasn't making the best sense. Have you never been confronted with something so terrible that even though the facts couldn't be plainer, you fight off recognizing them for what they are? You refuse to believe. Where there is clearly no hope you go on clinging to hope. I knew he was dead, but I didn't want to know it. I was postponing the onset of the full pain by pretending to myself that maybe if I got him a doctor quickly enough he could still be saved. You know, one of those medical miracles, making his heart beat again."

That much was drawn out of Dryden easily. The remainder of the process was slow and painful. Dryden insisted he knew nothing. Although he almost conceded that for anyone who had been so close to Ralph Henderson this ignorance he was now professing seemed hardly natural, he quickly followed the near-concession with an argument designed to erase it.

He had always felt it an essential part of his job to keep himself fully informed of all the affairs and concerns of Ralph Henderson —both personal and professional, private and public. When Henderson, however, made a clear and deliberate choice and it became obvious to Dryden that an area had developed in the Henderson affairs which his friend and employer chose to keep private even from Dryden, then Dryden considered that in this special area it was equally his obligation to refrain from seeking knowledge and even to blind himself and deafen himself to any clues that might happen to come his way.

"I can't say I didn't sense that there was something going on," he said, "or that it was something that had Mr. Henderson badly worried, but I hadn't a clue to what it was and, since I could see that he wanted it that way, I made a special point of knowing nothing about it."

"You can hardly feel compelled to go on not knowing now," Gibby told him.

Dryden sighed. "I don't know that I feel any less compelled," he said. "Whatever I do now, I'd like it to be what he would have wanted me to do, but it hardly makes any difference. After all, it is too late for me to ask him any questions."

"And there's no other source?" Gibby asked.

"If he didn't tell me what was worrying him, I hardly think he would have told anyone else."

"Crown?"

"It may be vanity, but I don't think he would take Mr. Crown into his confidence if he was barring me out."

"On an office matter? Crown was his partner."

Even the question seemed to give offense. Dryden didn't take kindly to the suggestion that anyone in any respect might have had any knowledge of Ralph Henderson that he himself hadn't had.

"Crown," he sneered. "He's never known his own business, much less any of Ralph Henderson's. But if you think it'll be worth anything, why don't you ask him?"

"We have."

"And?"

"*De mortuis nil nisi bonum,*" Gibby said. "He knows but he's not talking. It's enough that he destroyed Henderson. He's not going to destroy Henderson's good name as well."

Dryden exploded. "The rat," he snarled. "He said that?"

"He implied it."

"It's the same as saying it. Speak nothing but good of the dead and then he clams up leaving you with what to infer? That there isn't anything good that can be said of Ralph Henderson. The best day little Everett will ever know he won't be one tenth of the man Ralph Henderson was even in his worst hour."

Gibby picked up the worst-hour bit. "Which was what?" he asked.

Dryden wasn't answering. He just told us to go back to Crown. He guaranteed a breakdown in Crown's reticence.

"He's in shock now," he said, "or he ought to be. A man makes that kind of mistake and ends up killing the best friend he's ever going to have. That's enough to shake anyone up, even a mean little twerp like Everett Crown. But give him a day to bounce back, or even an hour or two, and he'll be babbling for you. He'll revert to type all right. With Everett Crown any silence you get is going to be merely temporary."

"And that's the way you want us to get it," Gibby said. "The way we'll have it from him, as nasty as possible."

Dryden groaned. "It's over and done with," he said. "What was was and nothing can change it now. Bring it out and it'll be nasty, no matter how you tell it. There's no way it can be anything but, except if you let it die."

"And a kidnapper just goes free?"

"With what?" Dryden countered. "He didn't get the ransom. The kid's back unharmed. Why can't it stop right here?"

"Because it was still a kidnapping. Forget Henderson. Henderson's out of it. We still need the kidnapper."

"I don't know anything about the kidnapper."

"But you do know what led up to the kidnapping. Give us that. We'll take it from there. It's somebody in your office."

"You know that? Then you know more than I do."

"Not more than you know, Dryden, only more than you're telling us."

"Okay then. You tell me."

"There's a shortage over at Henderson and Crown," Gibby said. "Somebody's had a hand in the till. It was fifty thousand dollars' worth or it may have been something less than that. At this stage there is no way of knowing just how ambitious the kidnapper was. Maybe he was just out to cover the shortage. Maybe he was aiming at something more than that, a little profit he could keep."

Dryden winced. "It's bad enough the way it is," he wailed. "Don't build it up. It was more than the fifty thousand. Fifty-one five to be exact. He was getting up the fifteen hundred some other way. He wasn't taking a cent more than he absolutely had to."

If Gibby felt any triumph in having opened up that chink in Dryden's defenses, he didn't let it show. He just went along with it as though he and Dryden might have been working the thing out cooperatively. It was not the moment for one-upmanship.

"It's a detail," he said. "In any event he kidnaps the Crown boy and he sets the ransom at a figure that will take care of that part of the shortage he can't cover otherwise, but that isn't enough. He gets the money and he makes restitution. Restitution, however, replaces the money but it doesn't obliterate the fact that for a period of time the money wasn't where it should have been. Along with the money coming back, the books have to be doctored to remove any evidence of its ever having been out."

"And that's what I walked in on when I dropped around to the office last night," I added. "He had been in there doctoring the books. He had to get out of there without my seeing him, and just getting out wasn't enough. There was more to be done before the night was out and I had to be prevented from raising an alarm. I had to be kept quiet and out of touch until he had accomplished the rest of it—returning the child, collecting the ransom, and I suppose returning to the office and stowing the fifty-one thousand five hundred in the safe."

I fired that straight at Dryden. The times fitted and so did the other factors. The wig and whiskers and the fancy dress, all the trappings that so emphatically negated the man's office look. I wasn't for a moment believing that they had been for his girl. I had conjured up for myself a far more reasonable explanation of the disguise.

Dryden, I was convinced, had put all that stuff on against the possibility that while returning the child and picking up the ransom he might be seen. He would, after all, if seen, have been visible only as little more than a silhouette dimly glimpsed in the murk. It had, of course, been a disguise that would have fooled no one who knew him well and who could see him clearly in a lighted place, but in the time and place set up for the exchange of child for money nobody was going to get any clear sight of him. The wig and sideburns and bell bottoms would have sufficed.

There was also the possibility that the disguise might have been enough to fool the child. Could wig and sideburns explain little Ralphie's silence when he'd been picked up from his crib?

I was watching Dryden closely. I was certain there would be a telltale reaction even if it would be nothing more than a visible increase in wariness. There was a reaction but nothing I would have expected.

"Only the fifty thousand collected in ransom," he said. "He had already put the fifteen hundred in there at the time when he cooked up the books. He'd already done that when you walked in on him or at least before he left you tied to the stairs."

So it wasn't what I'd expected. It didn't matter. It looked even better.

"How do you know?" I asked.

"You had me check," he answered, and he spoke without turning even a crewcut hair. "You had me open the safe. I saw then that figures had been changed in the books—a fifty-one five change—and that there was fifteen hundred in there that hadn't been there when I locked up in the afternoon."

"It's a detail," Gibby said. "It changed nothing. The whole thing still works out." He turned to me. "The peculiar way he handled you when you were fighting in the dark. It seemed as though he was playing with you, sadistically prolonging the struggle when he could have put you away quickly with one good punch. He had to do it that way because he had to dispose of you and come away from it showing not the slightest mark on himself. A puffed set of knuckles would have been enough to give him away when he would have to show himself later. He couldn't risk a punch."

That's Gibby for you. All he had to go on was what I had told him of that long and crazy struggle in the dark, but where I had let this bit of the thing slip my mind Gibby had latched on to it.

It's the way he works. Nothing is ever dismissed as inexplicable. What can't be explained sits at the front of his mind until it has satisfactorily been worked into the pattern of the crime.

I played along on it, gazing fixedly at Dryden's hands all the time Gibby was talking. Dryden didn't for a moment fail to notice it. This was a young man who never missed out on much. He spread his hands for inspection.

"I'll be just one of millions who threw no punches last night."

"How many of those millions," I asked, "had access to the safe? How many were in a position to cook up the books?"

Dryden shrugged it off. "Not many," he said. "In fact hardly any."

"The two partners and yourself," Gibby said. "Who else?"

Dryden squirmed. Obviously here was a question that struck uncomfortably close to the bone. There was a pause during which, on my guess, Dryden was casting around in his mind for some answer he could safely give. When eventually he did speak, it seemed evident that he'd failed to find one.

"I think you'll have to ask Mr. Crown that," he said. "He's the only one left who might be able to answer it competently."

"You don't know?" Gibby pressed him.

"Mr. Henderson, Mr. Crown, and myself," he said. "Beyond that I don't know, but I'm not prepared to say there isn't someone else. One or both of them may have given someone else access to the safe without informing me. One or the other of them may have been just that bit careless about letting someone see them work the combination. That way, of course, someone could have access without any of us knowing it. There are also people who can handle safes without knowing the combination. They sandpaper their fingertips or have I been looking at too much TV?"

"Choan, your job, and TV too," Gibby said. "You lead a busy life."

"Keeps me out of mischief," Dryden said.

"Or in," I told him.

It didn't seem possible that he could be missing the implication, but he took it to be disapproval of nothing more specific than the whole of his life style.

Gibby turned him back to the safe combination.

"Speaking just for yourself," he asked, "you are certain you were never careless about letting anyone see you open the safe?"

"To that I can swear."

Dryden gave it not even a moment's hesitation.

"And Crown will be able to answer for himself," Gibby said, "but who can answer for Henderson? Generally speaking, was he careless about things like that? Was he a trusting type?"

Dryden gave it a full answer. He didn't want to take anything on himself, nothing like suggesting that he was the only one of the three who was properly prudent. Henderson & Crown, he explained, were the partners. It was their business and their money. It wasn't his.

"That's the nature of trust," he said. "A man is as careful as he chooses to be with his own or in a partnership with what is even partially his own. I, a trusted employee, have an obligation to be careful. For them it is only a question of how much they care."

"One partner's obligation to protect the assets of the other?" I said.

"I suppose," Dryden murmured. "Actually you should be talking to Mr. Crown about this. I can speak for myself and I can speak for Mr. Henderson. If Mr. Crown has been careless about protecting the combination, he may remember."

Gibby passed up the latter part of that. "How can you speak for Mr. Henderson?"

"He never went near the safe," Dryden explained. "Any time he wanted anything out of it or he had something he wanted put away, he just had me do it. If he ever did work the combo himself, it would have been some time out of office hours when he was in the office alone. I wouldn't be around."

"You wouldn't be around," Gibby said. "That doesn't mean there wouldn't be someone else around."

"Doesn't it?"

"You tell me."

He could, of course, hardly speak for any office affairs of which he had no knowledge. So far as he did know, however, Henderson did nothing in a business way unless he had the faithful Dryden at his side.

"If there was anything like that," he said, "I was never told about it and nothing touching on it ever appeared in records I handled."

"Like getting up the fifty thousand for the ransom yesterday?" Gibby suggested.

"Yes. Like that."

"You know nothing of the fifty thousand?"

"Nothing, but it stands to reason that I wouldn't."

"What reason?"

"No love lost between the Crowns and me. In anything that involved her precious baby, I'd be the last man Mrs. Crown would want to trust."

"Does the child know you?"

"Well enough so he yells his head off if I so much as come near him. It must be he reads my mind."

In all his talk this was the first thing he'd said that might have been aimed at clearing himself of suspicion and most peculiarly it was the first thing he said on which he showed any evidence of regret at having spoken. The minute he had the words out, he looked as though he were wishing he could take them back. I expected Gibby to take it as an opening and probe deeper in that direction, but instead he changed the subject.

"Yesterday," he said. "Did you put in the ordinary office day? The usual nine to five?"

"I come in at eighty-thirty."

"I'm interested in the afternoon," Gibby told him.

Dryden sighed. "I guess it's no good my trying to lie about it," he said. "I was in the office all afternoon. You'll be asking the rest of the staff, so it would be no good me trying to tell you I wasn't there all afternoon."

"No use at all."

Dryden looked totally miserable. "You know," he said. "I suppose there was never any chance you wouldn't know."

"It had to be," Gibby said. "On the evidence and on what you and the Crowns tell us, there was never any other possibility."

For a moment I had misgivings about the way Gibby appeared to be believing everything this slippery character had been telling us. The fact that the part of his story that was clearly self-serving was the part that he seemed to be telling the most reluctantly hardly seemed sufficient proof that he was telling the truth. If there was one thing certain about Allen Dryden it was that from beginning to end he had been putting on an act. I could have taken my oath on it that his every word and his every move had been all too shrewdly calculated.

Trying to arrive at some sort of understanding of Gibby's thinking, however, I had to recognize that it was in just those bits that did seem self-serving where he had offered the information which could most readily be verified. As he had himself indicated, there would be plenty of witnesses who could be asked whether or not he had on the previous day been away from the office at any time during the afternoon. Similarly nothing could be easier than to test out the way he said the Crown child reacted to him. Everett and his Mrs. had already told us as much, not to speak of little Ralphie's "bad man."

This was too smart a cookie to do any lying in areas where there could be no hope of making a lie stand up, and on that basis he had to be believed. I was forced to the conclusion that, as Gibby said, there was no other possibility.

The kidnapper had access to the Henderson & Crown offices, and more than that he had access to the office safe. Even more he had been in a position where he was able to embezzle Henderson & Crown funds and he had sufficient knowledge of the firm's procedures to enable him to doctor the books so that, once he made restitution, he could obliterate any record that would indicate there had ever been an embezzlement.

Along with all these attributes, he had others at least as uncommon. He knew his way around the Crown home well enough so that he could steal in, grab the kid, and make off with him successfully. He knew the Crown household routine well enough to time the kidnapping perfectly. He knew just what dose of soporific it would take to put the kid out for the desired length of time without harming the boy. Above all, however, he was someone the kid knew so well and liked so well that he would give the man no trouble even before the sleeping pill took effect; and, more than that, the kidnapper had to be someone who would have been so much an expected attendant at the boy's cribside that, when questioned afterward, the boy could be expected to come up with a name so impossible that no one could believe the child was not referring to some other occasion.

Actually that bit of the plot had worked even better. The interruption of the boy's afternoon nap had been no such uncommon occurrence that the boy would remember it and the nap had been interrupted by someone who was so much an expected visitor that the kid was not enough impressed by the event to remember anything of it past his interval of drugged sleep.

The boy yelled his head off if Dryden so much as came near him and in any event Dryden had been in the office and in the company of a plethora of witnesses at the time of the kidnapping. So there it was. With Dryden eliminated I could see the conclusion and I saw it as quite as inevitable as Gibby said it was. There was no one left but Ralph Henderson, and since Henderson was the kidnapper and since with no abstract interest in justice his secretary-friend and his partner would feel that there could be nothing to be gained from uncovering a dead man's every last sin, it was easily understandable that they would both be reluctant to give us the story.

As soon as the reasoning boiled it down to Ralph Henderson, the whole series of events clicked into place. Even the on-again, off-again play he had made with me I had no difficulty with fitting into the total picture. Henderson, playing about with company funds, hadn't done as well as he'd hoped. That's a common enough story. A man embezzles a little and it's to be only for a short time till he has pulled off some big deal, put the money back, pocketed the margin of profit, and nobody the wiser. But the big deal goes sour and he reaches the place where he either has to do something desperate to find the money or he must make a clean breast of it to his partner and throw himself on his partner's mercy.

For a man like Henderson that would be bitter medicine. Also, since his partner was Everett Crown, I could see where he might have found it impossible to throw himself on the mercy of such a mean little twerp. He hits on the idea of the kidnapping. He knows how he can take the boy and he sees it as a scheme that can bring no possible harm to anyone. He can dope the kid up safely because he knows about the time the boy was doped accidentally and from that episode he knows the child's optimum safe dose.

The child knows him and likes him and that means he can take little Ralphie without frightening or startling the boy. The rest is easy. He gives Crown the ransom instructions, pretending that the kidnapper has been using him as the contact. He even makes that memorandum of the ransom rendezvous to build his scene of instructions coming to him over the telephone and not out of his own head.

The rest is to be easy. Crown will drop the ransom money at the appointed place and he will hurry off into the bandshell to look for the boy where Henderson has told him he is to find the child after he's left the ransom. Henderson expects that Crown, once he has the drugged child in his hands, will stop for nothing. He will be rushing the boy to a doctor and, while Crown is busy with that, Henderson will nip in, pick up the ransom money, go back to the office, toss it into the safe and hurry home to be anxiously waiting at the telephone for Crown to call him with the glad news that all went well, that he has little Ralphie, and that the boy is going to be okay.

Then what had he been up to in his play with me? That had been part of his cover-up. He couldn't be certain that even after he had secured the fifty thousand, shoved it into the safe, and cooked up the records, Dryden or Crown or both would be fooled. There was too strong a possibility that one or the other would have been aware that there had been a shortage and that the ransom money had been used to make it good.

In that event he would have had the call he'd made on me to fall back on. He, too, had been aware of the shortage. He had come to me about it, but immediately afterward, when the child was kidnapped, he had thought better of bringing me into it. His story would have been that he had enlisted the aid of the DA's office, the proper thing to do in a matter of embezzlement. When, however, he had realized that they were up against no ordinary embezzler but a man so dangerous that he would even risk a kidnapping, he had quickly called me off.

The money didn't matter. No chances could be taken with the safety of the child. Even when the thing had been all over, he could have argued that the boy's safety was still the most important consideration. If the Crowns at that point wouldn't have been sufficiently impressed with the thought that there would be a continuing danger to little Ralph even after the ransom had been paid and the boy recovered, he could invent for them further messages from the kidnapper that would make them happy to keep the whole affair hushed up.

Imagine for yourself where he would have stood with reference to the Crowns. He would be the generous friend who helped them raise the money for the ransom and who was more than ready to take any losses, whether a company loss or a personal loss, rather than risk the safety of their child.

It would have looked to him like a failproof plan. He could have foreseen none of the things that had gone wrong with it. He had been so sure of it that when he went to the office, he had gone in leaving the door unlocked behind him because he had seen no danger there except in the possibility of someone in the neighborhood seeing him slip in and out, and he could hardly have explained to Crown what he had been doing in the office when he had presumably been home standing by the phone for messages from the kidnapper. He had no choice but to go in and come out. He was going to have to do it twice in the course of the night, but each time he wanted it to be as quick as possible without any needless stopping for locks.

There was the one time he had to take the risk of hanging about on the doorstep fussing with locks and that was the first time he went in there. That was unavoidable but, while he was taking that necessary risk, he could cut down on future risks by fixing the door so that it was not locked at all. That way he was going to be able to slip out quickly and later, after collecting the ransom, he could return and slip in quickly. After that, on departure, it would be quite all right if he stopped to lock up properly.

If seen at that stage, he could have said that, having suspected all along that the purpose of the ransom had been for covering the company shortage, he had popped in there to see if the money had been returned. You might be wondering whether he couldn't just as easily have told the same story if he ran into anyone while stuck at the door unlocking locks. Of course he could, but it would have been a dangerous interruption, since then he would still have had the ransom money on him and he would have wanted to get it off his hands and into the safe as quickly as possible.

So then things started going wrong for him. I turned up and I had to be taken out of play till he had completed his night's work. He had managed me well enough, but then he did have to run the very risks he had been bent on avoiding. In order to make certain that he had me adequately secured, he did have to go through the whole business of locking the door after himself even on his first departure from the office. He would have been expecting to repeat the risks by standing on the doorstep and fiddling with all the unlocking when he would return with the ransom money. He'd had no choice. He could take no chances on leaving me insufficiently secured.

Actually at that point he'd played in luck. He took care of me and he left the offices unseen. It was the other unforeseeable development that did him in. Crown went to the rendezvous armed, and Crown was just that bit more mean-spirited than Henderson had recognized. Crown was torn between the money and the safety of his son. He had paused to glance over the parapet for a last regretful look at the fifty thousand and he'd seen the shadowy figure of the kidnapper as he came to pick up the money. Not recognizing the shadowy figure as Ralph Henderson, he aimed and fired.

Under the circumstances, when Gibby suggested turning Dryden loose, I had no objections. There was nothing to hold him for. Crown, of course, was not all that simple a matter. It was not in our province to drop all charges against him. We were going to have to go through the routine on him, but since there could hardly have been a case that bore more of the earmarks of justifiable homicide, we had no reason for holding him. We turned him loose on his own recognizance and the way he was talking even after Gibby broke him down to the point where he corroborated the story as I've already lined it out for you, it seemed impossible that there could ever be a judge or a jury that would condemn him as he was condemning himself.

He insisted that if he had only known, he would have been glad to play along with Henderson. First he bewailed the fact that Henderson hadn't just come to him and told him about the shortage. Then he berated himself for ever having paused for that look down at the kidnapper.

So there it seemed to be. Except for the more or less routine legal moves it was going to take to clean up the routine charges that had to be lodged against Crown, it would be a case closed. To my astonishment, however, even though he had unraveled the whole twisted story, Gibby wasn't satisfied. He ordered a tail put on Allen Dryden and he wanted it intensive.

"Now what is that for?" I asked.

"That Dryden," Gibby answered, "is a slippery type. You can't believe a word he says."

"That's neither here nor there," I argued. "On every point that matters he couldn't have more solid corroboration."

I have never felt on as secure ground as I did there. What both Dryden and the Crowns had told us of the way the Crown child reacted to him we had tested out even though we'd had a time persuading Mrs. Crown to permit us to bring Dryden together with little Ralph.

"I've never known what he did to the baby," she said. "He insists he did nothing, but Ralphie is terrified of him. The child has been through enough and Allen must have done something. Ralphie isn't a timid child and he likes people, but not Allen Dryden."

After much coaxing, however, she did consent and the demonstration couldn't have been more conclusive. At sight of Dryden the kid climbed into his father's arms and clung there in trembling terror. When, on Gibby's instructions, Dryden advanced toward the child and reached for him, little Ralphie let out the most ear-piercing screams, and they couldn't even begin to quiet him until Dryden was out of the room and the door firmly shut behind him. Even then it was some time before the kid's yelling subsided.

The check on the other point—Dryden's statement that he had not been out of the office all through the whole afternoon of the kidnapping—had been less dramatic, but in every member of the office staff from top to bottom he had a supporting witness and we hadn't gone far with questioning the office people before it became evident that Allen Dryden had been too much a power in the organization to have been popular and that he had used his power with so much heavy-handed arrogance that he had nothing but enemies in the place. They would have been glad of a chance to hang him, but they couldn't. He'd told the truth. He hadn't left the offices at any time that afternoon, not even for a moment.

I reminded Gibby of all this but, nevertheless, he insisted on the tail.

"Sure," he said. "Where he had to tell the truth he did, but virtually everywhere else he lied. Keeping an eye on him, we can't lose."

I wasn't so sure about that. The DA's office isn't so lavishly budgeted that we can waste costly man hours on pointless surveillance, but it didn't take many man hours.

It was that same night, shortly after midnight, when Gibby got the word. Dryden had left his apartment and, even though it was just about the time he might have been sallying forth to meet what he called that actress choan of his on the completion of her evening's performance, he had gone out without any of the appurtenances he'd declared essential for holding her interest—no bell bottoms, no wig, no sideburn pasties, nothing but his close-cropped, clean-shaven, uptight office look.

Gibby was kept advised of his movements and was enough interested to insist that he and I pull out and head in Dryden's reported direction. When we were en route in a police car and were told over the radio that Dryden had gone directly to Forty-second Street and that most unsavory block of it that lies just east of Eighth Avenue, I began wondering about the possibility that Dryden was beset by vices that even Gibby hadn't attributed to him.

When we got there, however, and connected up with his tail, we were told that he had gone into one of the all-night movie houses that are the most innocent feature of that neighborhood and had settled himself in the first row of the balcony.

We went in and went up to the balcony. Dryden was there as advertised. Even from the top of the steeply descending balcony aisle—and it was up there at the top that we stayed, going no closer to our quarry—he was easy to pick out.

You may be wondering about that, but then it's most unlikely that you've ever been in the balcony of one of those all-night cinemas. I don't think you'll find many readers among the patrons up there. They aren't even movie viewers.

They come in couples to sit in the dark and make love. They come singly in the hope of finding a coupling so that they might sit in the dark and make love. They come for no purpose at all except to get off the street. They come to sleep, to suck on a bottle, to smoke pot.

Whichever of these activities they may have come for, the occupants of the balcony want to be inconspicuous. They want to disappear into the murk of the darkened house. For that reason they always take seats about midway in the balcony. They avoid the back where the little lights over the fire-exit doors might cast some small revealing glow down on them, and they avoid the front where their heads and shoulders would silhouette against the background of the screen.

So down there in the front row Dryden sat alone. His was the only head and his the only shoulders silhouetted against the screen. As I said, we didn't go down the balcony aisle to join him. We remained at the top, where we had a good view of him. Gibby shoved me into a seat on one side of the aisle and took the seat across the aisle for himself.

"Sit tight," he whispered. "Don't declare yourself. Don't move until I do. He'll commit himself but only if we play it cool and wait for it. Before we take him, we want him irrevocably committed. He's slippery and he has a quick eye for loopholes. We don't want to leave him any."

I did as he told me. There wasn't much else I could do. I've never been more lost and yet it was obvious that Gibby hadn't suddenly gone out of his skull. Gibby did have something going for him whether I had a clue to it or not. A man doesn't pick himself up in the middle of the night and go down to Forty-second Street to sit on display in the balcony of one of those dirty old movie theaters.

If you go by the marquees outside, you might be deluded into expecting something sensational on the screen, but all the sensations are in the posters. The movies are all oldies, antiquated Westerns and vintage gang stuff. They were class-B turkeys even when they were new, the sort of junk that in the days of the double features always came as the other picture. Nobody has to go out to catch those. You can bring them in on your own TV screen any night you want to stay up late enough.

So Dryden wasn't there for the movie and he wasn't there for love. That he was there for something was obvious, and Gibby appeared to know what it was going to be. I could only make guesses. It was going to be a meeting of some sort. Sitting where he was, alone in the first row, he couldn't have been easier to spot. He had to be waiting for someone to join him and I sat there ignoring the bang-bang Western that thundered from the screen. As I stared at his back, I worked at rethinking the evidence that had cleared him of the kidnapping.

He had the two items going for him, his alibi and the way the child reacted to him. The alibi was unassailable, but did the alibi mean much once you began thinking in terms of this secret meeting he appeared to be waiting for? Dryden handled the office end of the job while an accomplice handled the actual snatch. Things had gone wrong. The deal had gone sour and now they would be meeting to talk it over. Exchange recriminations? Plan their next move? Check over their situation to make certain that they were going to be completely safe and that any door that might lead to suspicion of them had been properly sealed off by pinning the crime on a dead man?

I thought I was coming to a place where I might be beginning to make sense of the thing, but then I started chewing over Gibby's instructions and I was again at a loss. We were not going to make any premature move. We were going to wait till he had committed himself irrevocably without even the first loophole through which he might again slip away from us.

Since I could see nothing that might be coming up except a meeting, I was trying to figure how any meeting could do this good tight job of pinning guilt on our man. Was Gibby expecting Dryden to meet some known pro in the kidnapping game, someone so well known to us that the association would of itself be automatically incriminating?

It seemed to me that it would have to be that unless in some way Gibby had come up with a certainty that the meeting had been set up for the purpose of exchanging recriminations. I played about with that possibility. I couldn't see how Gibby could have any certainty about it and he did seem completely certain. Except for this one doubt, however, the idea did look good. It would fit with his instructions. We would sit tight till we had Dryden irrevocably committed. That sounded as though Gibby was expecting the meeting to explode into violence and we would be waiting for that moment of explosion before we would move in.

Then he came. I didn't see him come because I was concentrating on watching Dryden. If with some unidentifiable sense I hadn't become aware of Gibby's sudden tensing in his seat across the aisle, it might have been over before I'd even known it had begun. I did, however, sense it and I turned my head in time to see the revolver go up and take dead aim at Dryden where his head and shoulders were clearly silhouetted against the background of cowboys and Indians on the screen.

Gibby moved. I was poised to move with him. From the way he came up out of his seat I could tell that he would be coming in high. That had to mean he was going for the gun. That was all right. Gibby and I had been there before and it almost always divides up the same way. Gibby goes for the weapon. He leaves me the ankles. He says that working his way through school he didn't have much time for football. Usually a rolling block is the most effective way for me to go in, but not at the top of that steeply stepped balcony aisle. I would have had to roll uphill and that takes too much doing.

I dived at him headlong and I was lucky enough to hit just that fragment of a second after Gibby had come in under his gun arm. Gibby's onslaught had put him just a trifle off balance. He had begun staggering backward. So when I made contact, I was going his way but at a greater rate of speed and with more force.

What could easily have been a murderous tangle along the steep cant of that balcony aisle turned instead into a relatively simple and easily controllable scramble on the flat of the promenade behind the balcony. It was one of the noisier moments in the movie, what with the thunder of the hoofs of the Indian ponies and the barking of the U.S. Cavalry rifles.

Gibby drove the gun upward while I was wrapping my arms around the man's ankles and bringing him down. I don't know that I would have been at all aware of the shot that went off even as I was taking him if it hadn't all been at such close quarters that the revolver shot did assert itself in my ears as something quite different from the sound-track gunfire. On the screen Indians were biting the dust. Up on the theater ceiling, which in a better day had been painted with pink clouds and pinker *amoretti*, a soot-grimed cherub took the bullet that had been intended for Dryden. I fear the blackened *amoretto* was mortally wounded.

It was so quick and so drowned out by the din from the sound track that the balcony patrons, whether amorous or somnolent, never even noticed. Dryden, however, having been tense and alert for his meeting with Everett Crown, was quick to register on it. He came charging up the aisle and, by the time we had Crown disarmed, under control, and backed off the balcony into the upstairs lobby, Dryden was at our side.

As Gibby had foreseen, Crown was quick to reach for a loophole.

"Okay," he said. "Okay. I know. I haven't the right to take the law into my own hands, but a man can stand only so much. This louse was in it with Ralph all along. I could have forgiven Ralph, but I made the big mistake and now it's too late. Ralph is gone and Dryden I'll never forgive. I told him to meet me here. I told him to take a seat in the front row. I told him it was so I could spot him when I came in and we could get together easily. Sure, I set him up, but he had it coming."

"He did have it coming," Gibby agreed. "Blackmailers always have it coming, but stack blackmail up against cold-bloodedly planned, deliberate murder and blackmail becomes just another little nothing."

"I admit it," Crown said. "I have been planning to murder Dryden, but he had it coming. It's his fault that Ralph's dead. It's his fault that my wife will never draw an easy breath again. Do you know what it is to have your kid taken for ransom? Do you know what it is to go through those hours of not knowing whether somebody's hurting him or even of not knowing whether you'll ever see him alive again?"

"We bleed for you," Gibby told him. "Henderson found the shortage. He suspected you, but he didn't want to believe it. He came to Mac, hoping that with a pro looking at it, he was going to be told he was wrong. Then you told him little Ralph had been kidnapped and that the kidnappers said they would deal only through him."

I caught it. "Yes," I said. "Ralph Henderson was no fool. He matched the figures up. Fifty thousand ransom came significantly close to the amount of the shortage, but the shortage had lost its importance. The kidnapped child was all that mattered, and he had to call me off. Until the child had been recovered he didn't want anybody looking at that shortage."

"Right," Gibby said, never turning away from Crown. "Henderson helped you with raising the fifty thousand. Henderson waited for the word on where he was to deliver it. You called him and told him that the kidnapper had contacted you with the instructions. They were your instructions, of course, but you told Henderson that they wanted him to deliver the ransom and you set it up for him to put himself in exactly the right spot alongside the bandshell. That was the one bit of the scheme that never did make sense, the kidnapper letting you have the child before he had the ransom. That's not the way kidnappers work."

"It's always that they get the ransom," I said, "and then maybe you get the child."

"Of course, when you're your own child's kidnapper and you're handing him back to yourself," Gibby said, "you have the child before the ransom is paid because you've had the child all along. Nothing could be simpler. You go up into the bandshell with your doped-up baby. You wait for Henderson to come and leave the ransom money at the appointed place. He bends over to set it down and you're zeroed in on him from the bandshell. Nothing could be easier. A man is shot when he is bending over to put a package of money down. No examination of his body will ever tell us that he wasn't shot when bending over to pick it up."

"He had the thing all figured," Dryden said. "He'd kill Ralph. He'd already have cooked the books to hide the fact that there had ever been a shortage, but you can never really hide a thing like that and he knew it. The effect would be that there had been the shortage. Someone had cooked the books in anticipation of making restitution and Ralph Henderson is killed when he is picking up the money that would be used for the restitution. That's better than relying on nobody noticing the monkey business with the figures. There was a shortage. It was Ralph's shortage. He tried to make it good with the kidnapping. He died for it. Crown not only framed Ralph Henderson for his own embezzlement. He murdered him just to make the frame stick."

"And what part did you play in all this?" I asked.

Dryden waved the question aside. He was having second thoughts about what he'd just been saying.

"No," he said. "It wasn't just to make the frame stick. It was good for more than that. Crown is sitting pretty with the whole of Henderson and Crown in his hands. Check Ralph Henderson's will. Little Ralph is big Ralph's heir. Neat, wasn't it?"

"Very neat," Gibby agreed. "We question the boy. We ask him who took him up from his afternoon nap and we get no answers but Mummy and Daddy. There's no way to figure that except for the kid talking about afternoon naps in general, and he's too young to separate one nap from all the other naps since there was nothing so startling about being picked up by good Uncle Ralph, but it wasn't Uncle Ralph. Even less startlingly, it was Daddy."

"Neat," Dryden agreed, "but he figured without me. I knew about the shortage all along and I knew who lifted the money."

He was beginning to be too proud of himself. Gibby kicked that in the teeth.

"You knew? Why didn't you tell Henderson what you knew?"

"Tell Henderson about this louse?" Dryden jerked his head in Crown's direction. "I was going to need airtight proof before I said a word to Henderson. He loved this jerk like a brother. It wasn't going to be easy to convince him."

"Far easier to sit back and watch Crown get himself in deeper and deeper," Gibby said, "until he would have himself so deeply mired that you could blackmail him, and good. You didn't tell Henderson and even when the thing had escalated to murder, you didn't tell us. You were still out for blackmail. Crown didn't tell you to come here and set yourself up in the front row and you didn't come just for nothing. You've never been anybody's patsy."

I caught Gibby's reasoning. Just as Crown had reversed the thing in his story, telling us that the kidnapper negotiated through Henderson with Henderson relaying the instructions to Crown when actually the messages had been going the other way with Crown telling Henderson where to go and what to do, he had now tried to work the same switch on us again.

I put it to Crown. "You didn't tell Dryden to come here," I said. "He told you. He called you and set up this meeting. He told you to come here and buy his silence and you pretended to be eager to go along with his demands. You told him to set himself up in the front row so you could find him easily to pay him off. You just didn't specify the kind of payoff you had in mind."

"I should have known," Dryden said. "He shot his best friend. Why should he stop at me? I should never have trusted the rat."

"Bad judgment," Gibby said, "but that's the way it goes. There's nothing like greed for warping a man's judgment."